S0-BEP-888

Finding
Anna Bee

Finding
Anna Bee

Cindy Snider

Illustrated by
Mary Chambers

Herald Press

Scottdale, Pennsylvania
Waterloo, Ontario

Library of Congress Cataloging-in-Publication Data
Snider, Cindy Gay, 1948-
  Finding Anna Bee / Cindy Snider ; illustrated by Mary Chambers.
      p. cm.
  Summary: Anna Bee and her five new friends at church summer
camp find a mysterious doorway to the past and learn first hand
about Anabaptist faith heroes as well as discovering much about
themselves, each other, and the importance of peace.
  ISBN 978-0-8361-9392-3 (pbk. : alk. paper)
  1. Mennonites--Juvenile fiction. [1. Mennonites--Fiction.
2. Time travel--Fiction. 3. Church camps--Fiction. 4. Camps--
Fiction. 5. Christian life--Fiction. 6. Friendship--Fiction. 7. Self-
perception--Fiction.] I. Chambers, Mary, ill. II. Title.
  PZ7.S6801Fin 2007
  [Fic]--dc22
                                                    2007017778

FINDING ANNA BEE
Copyright © 2007 by Herald Press, Scottdale, Pa. 15683
Published simultaneously in Canada by Herald Press,
Waterloo, Ont. N2L 6H7. All rights reserved
Library of Congress Catalog Card Number: 2007017778
International Standard Book Number: 978-0-8361-9392-3
Printed in the United States of America
Book design by Merrill R. Miller
Cover art and illustrations by Mary Chambers

12 11 10 09 08 07   10 9 8 7 6 5 4 3 2 1

To order or request information, please call 1-800-245-7894,
or visit www.heraldpress.com.

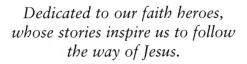

Dedicated to our faith heroes,
whose stories inspire us to follow
the way of Jesus.

Contents

Acknowledgments

With appreciation to friends, family, and mentors whose gifts of encouragement, feedback, chocolates, and coffee helped bring Anna Bee and her friends to life.

Special thanks to Roberta Harms, Harold Thieszen, Coleman and Susan Cooper, Cindy Mines, Linda Blain, and Bonnie Tharp. And much gratitude to Mary Clemens Meyer, editor extraordinaire, and Eleanor Snyder, who initiated and guided the publication of this book.

1

Hot Jokes

It all started on the hottest day Alicia Aduma could remember. She knew she was born on the hottest day on record, but that was 12 years ago. Today was so hot that Alicia's little brother, Justin, and their 13-year-old neighbor, Isaac Thomas Roth, were making up stupid "hot jokes."

"It's so hot the blue jays have to chill the worms they pull out of the ground," Isaac Thomas teased Justin. "Otherwise, they'd burn their throats when they swallowed them."

Justin laughed, but Alicia rolled her eyes.

"It's so hot that my super-size, blue raspberry slush has to sit under a shade tree and fan itself," added Justin with a grin.

Isaac turned to him and made a proposal. "It's so hot I bet we can fry an egg on the sidewalk in front of your house."

"It's so hot I'm going to scream if either of you tells another 'hot joke!'" Alicia moaned, rolling her eyes again.

Isaac winked at Justin. "Let's lose the jokes and hit the sidewalk, bro. Got an egg?"

Justin ran to the kitchen and brought back two eggs, a plate, and a spatula. The two boys—Isaac, tall and lean with a mop of long brown hair, and Justin, short and stocky with close-cut, wiry curls—took their supplies outside. Alicia watched the experiment from the front door.

After about five minutes, she saw Isaac and Justin scoop two fried eggs off the pavement and slap them onto the plate. They each grabbed an egg with their fingers, tossed back their heads, and plopped the mess into their open mouths.

"Gritty, but good," pronounced Isaac, smiling at Justin. He spoke louder than usual, so Alicia would be sure to hear.

"Very good, even with that little ant in mine," Justin agreed.

"Yuckola!" yelled Alicia. "How can boys be so gross?"

She would always remember the egg-frying episode, but that sizzling hot summer would stay in her mind for other reasons. It was the summer they met a moving mass of hot and bothered honey bees. It was the summer they got caught up in mysterious vines that led them to a carousel, a castle, and other strange places. And it was the summer they met the craziest-haired, wildest girl ever.

2

Hot Bees

The crazy-haired girl pedaled down the sidewalk on her bike, lickety-split toward the Aduma house. Alicia, Justin, and Isaac could see her bleach-streaked dreadlocks flying around her head. She was standing up on the pedals, her legs pumping wildly.

The girl was screaming words they couldn't understand till she got closer. "Let the bees pass! Let the bees pass! Don't hurt 'em!"

That's when Alicia saw the gray, pulsating cloud moving toward them. She hesitated, trying to make sense of everything—the loud buzzing sound, the frantic girl on the barreling bicycle, the moving mass of something—all heading straight for them.

"Get out of the way! Get out of the way!" she yelled, flinging her arms toward Isaac and Justin. "There's a crazy girl and thousands of bees heading for us!"

They ran for the big lilac bush in the front yard and dove under its cover. That's when Alicia's dad came running out of the house and collided with the

hot-and-bothered swarm of honey bees. And that's
when the crazy-haired girl came to a screeching halt.

"Get up! Get up!" she cried, dropping her bike to
the pavement beside Alicia's dad. "They didn't mean
to hurt you! They got hot! They got loose! I couldn't
net 'em! Are you allergic to bee stings? Are you a
policeman? Are you okay?"

Alicia ran up to help her dad, who was sprawled
on the sidewalk with his arms cradling his head and
ears. The crazy-haired girl was covered with sweat.
"Call an ambulance! Call an ambulance *now*!" she
screamed.

When the medics arrived, they said it was a good thing Alicia's dad wasn't allergic to bee stings.

"Two hundred stings to the head, neck, and arms," the doctors told him. His whole head was red and swollen, and his neck and arms looked like a sumo wrestler's. The doctors advised an overnight stay at the hospital.

"I'm so mad at that crazy girl I could spit," Alicia told Justin. She grimaced watching Dad struggle to drink a cup of water through his swollen lips. "I can't wait to tell her parents," she said. "I'm sure *she's* not going to. Why else would she ask if Dad was a police-man?"

3

Bee-Girl

L isten, Justin, Dad's going to be all right. Honest. Cross my heart and hope to die."

"Don't say that, Alicia! Don't say 'hope to die.' I don't want anyone else to die."

Justin was six years old when their Grandpa Will died and seven when their mom died. Dad had encouraged them to talk about their sad feelings. That was hard for Alicia, but not for Justin.

"I'm sorry, Justin. I won't say that ever again. Cross my heart and . . ." Alicia caught herself in mid-sentence. ". . . I mean, I promise. Forgive me?"

Justin didn't say anything, just looked at the floor.

Alicia spoke again. "Not even 200 nasty bee stings can keep our dad down. Bees can't sting the goodness out of him, either. He's just like you that way."

Justin looked up at Alicia and smiled. "I forgive you," he said.

"Guess what?" She changed the subject. "Dad wants you and me to find that crazy-haired bee girl, welcome her to the neighborhood, and invite her to church camp next week."

Justin's eyes lit up. "Really? That's awesome! I bet Bee Girl will love camp. Especially if we look for insects like we did last year. She'll be sizzling like a bee sting on a grill."

"Oh, brother, you've obviously been spending too much time with Isaac Thomas Roth. Why don't you help me find 1730 Crescent Street? That's the bee girl's address, Isaac said. Maybe you two can make friends with her, but I don't think she and I would get along. I'm certainly not interested in bees."

"How do you know she's interested in bees? Just because she was chasing them down the street?"

"Well, Justin dear, didn't you notice that her shorts and top had honey bees all over them? Along with her shoes, shoelaces, and wrist band. Plus there were honey bee stickers covering her entire bike. And, her black hair had bleached blond stripes that made it look like bee hair!"

"Really? Cool! I wish I *did* notice."

"Do guys ever notice anything?" Alicia rolled her eyes.

"I noticed that she looked special, like a bee girl should." Justin grinned.

"You and Dad are so alike—always finding good in everyone and everything, even if they hurt you. It's a nice trait, but pretty impractical."

The next day, when Dad came home from the hospital, his face was still swollen. His eyes looked like slits, surrounded by puffy tissue. It made Alicia want to cry, but she didn't. Justin ran to him with a big bear hug.

"Justin, be careful! You'll hurt Dad."

Dad opened his arms wider and motioned for Alicia to join them.

"I'm not *that* fragile," he laughed. "I just have a fat face. The emergency crew made sure I didn't go into shock. And I've got medicine to help the swelling go down. I'll be just fine."

He turned to Alicia. "Have you thought about my idea for inviting the 'bee girl' to church camp? God works in mysterious ways, you know. Maybe the bees will bring us another friend and bring that young lady and her family something good too. I think God can use those wayward bees and redeem my little bit of suffering, don't you?"

Alicia didn't say anything. She stared at Dad like it was the most preposterous thing she had ever heard.

He smiled. Justin broke the silence with a long string of questions. "What does *redeem* mean? Why were the bees rolled up in a ball? How did they get loose? Why didn't all of them sting you? Where are the bees now? Will somebody kill them? Did you report it to the police?"

Dad held up his hand. "Hey, slow down. Let's answer one question at a time. *Redeem* means to change something bad or negative into something of value and beauty. God can change my suffering from the bee stings into something worthwhile in the bigger scheme of things. Does that make sense to you?"

"Kinda. I'll have to think about it some more," Justin said.

"Well, it's a serious subject and worthy of a lot of

thinking," said Dad. "We'll talk about it again some-time. Now where were we with your list of questions?"

"Did you report it to the police?"

"No, I didn't call the police," smiled Dad. "And your other questions are really more suited for a bee expert. I think one lives in our neighborhood, as a matter of fact. The expert you may be inviting to church camp, remember?" He winked at Justin and Alicia.

"Okay, Justin, let's do it." Alicia tried to sound enthusiastic for Dad's sake. "Let's find Isaac Thomas and make a beeline for the bee expert."

"Hey, Alicia, I think Isaac's humor is rubbing off on you."

Alicia was rolling her eyes when they heard a knock at the front door. "I bet that's Isaac Thomas right now," she said.

"She's coming, Isaac, hold up!" Justin yelled.

Alicia opened the door and gasped.

"Good afternoon," greeted a tall, muscular man with deep-set eyes. His long black hair was tied back in a ponytail, and his skin was the color of chestnuts. "I'm Donald Running Strong, and this is my daughter . . ."

"I'm Anna Bee! And I'm here to apologize to your dad," interrupted the girl with yellow-black striped hair and piercing black eyes. Alicia noticed that her skin was lighter than her father's, and freckles dotted her nose and cheeks. Her apple red tank top sported flying bees every few inches.

"I'm . . . I'm . . . uh," Alicia stuttered. "My dad's inside. Wait just a minute."

Justin ran to the door, shouting, "Isaac Thomas, let's go redeem some bees . . ." His mouth fell open when he saw the girl with the bee-striped hair.

"I'm Anna Bee!" she told him. "And I'm here to apologize to your father."

The tall man stepped forward. "Hello, son. I'm Anna's father, Donald Running Strong. We're sorry about what happened yesterday, and we want to make things right."

"Happy to meet you," said Justin with a smile. "Do you want to come in? I'll get my dad."

Alicia and her dad almost collided with Justin as he rounded the hallway corner in a full run. "Dad, it's the bee girl, and she's got her dad with her!"

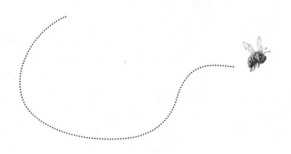

4

The Invitation

I can't believe Bee-Girl accepted our invitation to church camp," Alicia said, sighing and rolling her eyes. "People should know when they're not *really* welcome."

Isaac Thomas had joined her in the kitchen, where she was cooking soup for her dad.

"That's the good old community spirit for you," he said sarcastically. "Just what our ancestors—well, *my* ancestors—had in mind. You've been adopted into our great faith tradition, Alicia dear, welcomed into the great fold of Anabaptist martyrs, Mennonite peacemakers, community service workers, conscientious objectors . . ."

"Stop it, Mr. Model Mennonite! You might know all there is to know about Anabaptists and Mennonites, but I know how it feels to be an outsider. We'll welcome Anna Bee—if that really is her name, and we'll make sure everyone else at camp does too."

"That's the spirit! I, Isaac Thomas Roth, being of sound Mennonite mind and body, do hereby swear to cooperate in every way with Alicia Marie Aduma, who, being of somewhat sound mind, tries to be a faithful follower of Jesus Christ. We together promise to welcome one Anna Bee, of unknown rank and heritage, to our community of oneness and higher peace, to our great Camp Amani Ya Juu."

"Have you been looking at your mom's law books again, Isaac Thomas? Please try to communicate simply and forthrightly—oh no, you've got me using big words too," Alicia said, a smile twitching the corners of her mouth. "And Mennonites don't swear, Isaac Thomas. We let our 'yes' be 'yes' and our 'no' be 'no.' You should know that."

"Ah, yes, Alicia dear. Just testing to see if you learned your Anabaptist and Mennonite history during newcomers' class. I will be glad to recommend you to higher learnings and personally vouch for you before the illustrious Church Council of Camps and Covenants. Now let us go forth to win others into the community of our beloved camp."

"I think I'm going to throw up. But before I do, Isaac Thomas, promise you'll stop calling me 'dear.' I'm not a dear, and especially not *your* dear!"

"Come on, you guys!" Justin ran into the kitchen. "It's time to go to camp! Fabio and Li are waiting for us. And Anna Bee's on her bike. We're all going together."

"Well, is Bee-Girl going to escort us or something? I mean, why is she the only one riding a bike?"

"Alicia, stop calling her Bee-Girl," said Justin. "She said her name's Anna Bee."

"And you believe that?"

"Sure, that's what she said. Her dad's Native American and her mom was born in Ireland. Her dad is Donald Running Strong, and her mom is Elizabeth Bee. They moved here three weeks ago. She has a brother who's six. Her mom's in the military, and she's in prison."

Alicia and Isaac jerked their heads around and stared at each other, their eyes big as saucers and their mouths gaping.

"Her mom's in the military?" Isaac Thomas repeated.

"Her mom's in *prison*?" Alicia opened her eyes wider. "How do you know all this?"

"I talked to Anna yesterday when she and her dad came by. Come on, let's get to camp!" Justin turned and ran toward the door.

"This is going to be an interesting week, Alicia, my dear, an interesting week indeed."

Alicia slammed her foot onto Isaac Thomas's shoe. "Don't call me dear! Go ahead and follow Justin. I'll get my sandals and be right out. Ready or not, Camp Amani Ya Juu, here we come!"

5

Camp Amani Ya Juu

Welcome to Camp Amani Ya Juu, everyone!" greeted the four camp counselors, trying to get 30 campers to sit quietly on quilts scattered across the lawn. The park was in the middle of the city, with a small lake and a deep creek that wound along the gently sloping edges of the grass. There were lots of trees and rock outcrops and at least three bridges—perfect for a day camp.

"Everyone, listen up, please!" shouted the counselor with long blond hair. "I'm Christina. And this is Tim, Andi, and Jesse—your Camp Amani Ya Juu leaders for this week.

"Today is the first day of the rest of your life," she continued. "What are you going to do with it? Sleep all day? Sit at a television? Play video games for eight hours straight? Don't even think about it! Not today, not this week. You'll be doing something much more exciting!"

"Each day, you'll meet heroes," added Tim. "And we don't mean rap stars, movie celebs, or big-time sports heroes. You'll learn about people who died for what they believed in, for following the way of Jesus. It won't always be a pretty picture, campers. But we think you're ready. Ready to get to know your spiritual ancestors and learn from them."

"You'll learn about modern-day heroes too," added Andi. "Men and women and even kids like you who are following Jesus by serving others and taking a stand for peace."

Jesse spoke next. "*Amani Ya Juu* means 'higher peace' in Kiswahili. This week, you'll learn that Anabaptists live and work in all parts of the world. Their faith in God gives them, and us, a higher peace that goes beyond all kinds of differences.

"Campers, get ready for an exciting week! Each day we'll worship God, search the scriptures for some serious treasure, and get to know each other through fun activities. There'll be lots of surprises, too. So have fun, have faith, and follow your trusty camp counselors."

Alicia, Isaac, Li, Fabio, and Justin had found a quilt to sit on with some other campers. The five had been friends ever since Alicia and Justin started attending the Mennonite church. Alicia hadn't made friends as easily with the other kids at church. They seemed stand-offish, and she wondered if they didn't like her because she was black.

"Where did Anna go?" asked Justin.

Just then, Anna, sitting on the edge of another quilt, yelled out to the counselors, "Hey! Were any of those hero people jailbirds?"

Alicia hid her face. "I can't believe she said that."

"Yes, as a matter of fact, many of them were 'jailbirds' at one time or another," answered Christina.

"Why is Anna sitting over there by herself?" Justin asked.

"Because she feels like an outsider, that's why," answered Fabio.

"So, she's acting like one," added Li.

"Makes sense to me, dear friends," Isaac joined in.

"Well, she really *looks* like an outsider," said Alicia, "with those clothes. Army camouflage shorts and a T-shirt with a military aircraft that says 'Don't Mess with Mean.' At a peace camp? *Really!* I told her it was a Mennonite camp and that we'd be learning about Anabaptist faith heroes. You know what she said?"

"What?" the others asked in unison as they leaned toward Alicia.

"She said she wasn't interested in learning about anybody who was anti-Baptist. Before I could explain, she told me her mother's grandfather was a Baptist preacher, and even if her family didn't go to church any more, it wasn't right to be anti-Baptist."

"She's got a point there," Isaac laughed.

"Don't act dumb, Menno ace! You know very well what Anabaptist means. Even *I* know, and I didn't grow up Mennonite."

"What *does* it mean?" Justin chimed in.

"That's what you're going to find out this week," Alicia answered.

"I hope they don't scare the younger kids," Isaac

said. "Some of our Anabaptist ancestor stories can be pretty gory."

"What do you mean scare the younger kids? I'm eight, and I'm not scared of anything!" Justin proclaimed, scowling.

"Sorry, Justin, I didn't mean you're a coward. It's just that it might be a little much for some kids."

"Well, I'm sure they won't be teaching scary things at camp," Alicia replied. "That's for older sisters and brothers to do during ghost story time." She bared her teeth and lunged at Justin.

"I can't wait!" exclaimed Justin. "I love everything about camp—even the ghost stories."

"Hey, where's Anna Bee? She was just there, and now she's gone," whispered Li, as Christina and the other counselors prayed for God's blessing on the week.

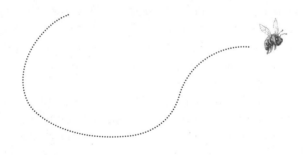

6

Finding Anna Bee

Follow me!" Fabio shouted, leading the rest of the Menno Fab Five, as they called themselves at camp. "I saw her run through the trees over there."

"Where's she going?" Alicia raised her voice. "She's going to ruin our week. We can't waste time trying to find her every time she runs off."

"I can't blame you for having a bad attitude toward her, Alicia," Isaac said. "She was kinda the reason your dad got hurt. But you did promise your dad you'd invite Miss Bee to camp. And you said you'd be welcoming, because you understood how being an outsider feels."

Justin sprinted ahead. The others set out in a slow run behind him, but he soon disappeared into the trees.

"I can't see Justin anymore," Alicia complained. "Now he's lost too. Which path do we take now?"

"Hey," Li said suddenly. "Look over there! That must be one of the bridges that was vandalized and then rebuilt—right through those trees with the hanging vines. I don't remember seeing those vines before."

"Neither do I," said Isaac. "Maybe they're there for a vine lesson."

"What do you mean, a 'vine lesson'?" Alicia asked. "Are you planning to teach us how to swing from the vines like Tarzan?"

"Aaa-aa-aa-aah!" Isaac yelled at the top of his lungs. "Me Tarzan, you Jane. Tarzan no want to swing on vine. Tarzan want to teach Jane lesson of vine. 'I am the vine, you are the branches; Apart from me, you can do nothing.' That's what Jesus said. John 15:5."

"Isaac the preacher man. You ought to find a Bible college, man. You know a lot about the Bible," said Fabio.

"That's exactly what I'm planning to do, bro. Unless God advises otherwise."

"Well, lead on Preacher Man," said Alicia. "We've got to find Justin and Anna, with or without a Bible."

"Dear friends, I have a sneaking suspicion that finding Anna Bee is going to be our primary mission this week. Like looking for a lost sheep. Are you ready for the adventure?" asked Isaac.

"Aye, aye. We are!" shouted Li and Fabio. Alicia rolled her eyes.

7

Crossing the Bridge

W ow, this new bridge is great, man." Fabio turned to Isaac. "The vines are covering the bridge like a tunnel to a jungle. How'd they get the vines to grow on the new bridge so fast? They're covering the whole thing—the sides, the floor, and even arching over the top."

Li took the first step onto the bridge as the others stared at the huge vine with its trumpet-shaped blossoms. "Look," she exclaimed, "There's an engraving down here on a stepping stone."

Li forced the vines apart, to see better. "That's weird. It's got strange-looking animals on it. And a man with a flute. Or is that a peace pipe he's blowing on?"

"Let me see," Isaac stepped on the bridge beside Li. "What's really weird is that this wooden bridge has stepping stones in its floor. That doesn't make sense. The weight of the stones could make the wood splinter and fall into the creek. Yep, this is a strange bridge we're on, dear friends. Maybe we're in the middle of a ghost story," he half-laughed.

"Would you guys stop? We are *not* in the middle of a ghost story." Alicia shook her head.

"But we're in the middle of something, that's for sure." Fabio was stooping down to take a look at the engraving. "That looks like some kind of Mayan drawing. I think it's a picture from the *Popol Vuh*."

"Say what?" Li, Isaac, and Alicia cocked their heads toward Fabio at the same time.

"The *Popol Vuh*," said Fabio. "The Mayan Book of the Dawn of Life."

"Now why would something from that book be in a place like Camp Amani Ya Juu, dear Fabio?" Isaac asked, saying aloud what everyone was thinking.

"God works in mysterious ways," Fabio answered. "The *Popol Vuh* is a magical book, full of imagination and creativity. My dad says it's a good book for Anglos to read, to understand Hispanic culture. Maybe you should read it to better understand me," he added, grinning.

"Well, we certainly need help in that area." Isaac grinned back. "Sometimes your ways are a real mystery, multi-cultured friend."

"You mean 'multicultural,' don't you, Isaac?" Alicia smirked. "I doubt you'd want Fabio as a friend if he were a multi-culture of something, like a bacteria culture and a fungi culture and a . . ."

"Okay, so that's the first vocabulary slip I've made in my entire 13 years. Build a bridge and get over it, Alicia dear."

"Can't stand not being perfect, can you, Isaac?" Alicia shot back.

Fabio suddenly stood up. "Hey, what happened to Li? Where'd she go?"

"I don't know. Please explain to me why people keep disappearing around here." Alicia frowned. "I can't see a thing through those vines. We have to find Justin!"

"Don't forget Anna Bee. She's the one we started out to find, remember?" Isaac walked faster, looking up at the bridge's trailing, cluttered vines and then down at its multicolored stepping stones. Alicia watched as he and Fabio disappeared through the wall of vines.

"Hey, wait up, guys! And watch out for the bees. I just saw some flying out of the blossoms."

But Isaac and Fabio didn't hear Alicia's warning about the bees. They were already in another world.

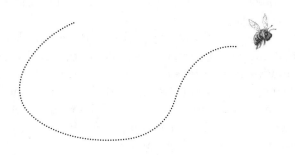

8

The Giant Carousel

What Alicia found on the other side of the bridge both startled and frightened her. She was alone, in the middle of a clearing with no vines, no trees, no grass. No Isaac, Fabio, Li, or Justin. And no troublemaker, Anna Bee.

What she saw was a giant carousel, moving slowly round and round. Beyond the painted horses, monkeys, swans, and huge rabbits were enormous hanging tapestries. The giant, colored cloths portrayed men with long hair, beards, and funny-looking hats. *Definitely from another era, but they look a little familiar,* thought Alicia.

"Alicia, Alicia, where are you?" She recognized Justin's muffled voice. It seemed to be coming from the carousel. *He must be behind one of the tapestries,* she thought. She hesitated for a moment, then hopped aboard the circling carousel. "Justin, Justin, where are you?"

Alicia flung herself against the first tapestry, the one with the blond, long-haired man, and looked up at his piercing eyes. "This is my story," he said as his soft, velvet lips parted. Alicia gasped and dove under the tapestry to the other side.

As she stood up, the bright sun momentarily blinded her. She wished she had brought the quilt along, for even though the sun was warm on her shoulders, she was shivering with cold. The bright sunlight, the cold, the shivering down her spine—they reminded her of the day of her mother's funeral. "I'm freezing," she said.

"Sh-h-h!" Isaac was two feet behind her, lying belly-down on the ground. Alicia jumped and turned around. He motioned to her. "Sh-h-h! Get down, or they'll see you!"

"*Who* will see me?" demanded Alicia, still standing. "What are you talking about? Where are Justin and the others? And why is it so cold? You're shivering too."

"Sh-h-h!" Isaac reached over and pulled at Alicia's legs. "Get down! Do you want them to throw you into that icy water?"

Alicia looked around more closely. There was white stuff on the ground everywhere. She slowly squatted down, feeling dazed and confused. Isaac held out a small, bare tree branch to her.

"Here, you can use this to clear the snow away, so you don't have to lie down on the ice. Please get down, Alicia, so no one can see you. I'm afraid we've entered another time and place. It's not morning, it's not Monday, and it's not summer anymore. We're not at camp, Alicia. It's three o'clock in the afternoon, Saturday, January 5, 1527, and we're in Zurich, Switzerland."

Alicia rolled her eyes. She could see what looked like snow and she could feel the frigid temperature, but what Isaac said made no sense at all.

"Isaac Thomas Roth, this is no time for jokes!" she hissed. "We've got to find Justin and the others and get back to the welcome celebration. The counselors will be looking for us. I don't want to get in trouble on the first day of camp."

"Alicia, I know this sounds crazy, but you have to believe me. We're on the banks of the Limmat River in Zurich, Switzerland. See that stone tower in the middle of the river?" Isaac looked out over the river and pointed to a tall tower, where people were milling about.

"Yes, I see it," Alicia answered. "It's just another thing they've added to the camp."

"Open your eyes, Alicia! Do you think those people over there in the long capes and funny-looking clothes are strolling camp actors?"

"Well, I guess so."

"No! They're here to see Felix Manz executed. Some of them are probably Zurich councilmen and church leaders, the ones who condemned him to death. All the others are here out of curiosity. That stone tower is the Wellenberg Prison, where they're holding Manz. Watch that tower, Alicia. The government authorities will be bringing Manz out any minute."

"Okay, Isaac, you're scaring me now. You're acting a little too weird. Are you on medication or something?"

"No, I'm not on medication. Okay, I took an allergy pill this morning . . . Stop changing the subject!" Isaac took a deep breath. He looked at Alicia and spoke more slowly, "Do you remember hearing about Felix Manz in the newcomers' class?"

"Yes. He was the first Anabaptist martyr. He was drowned in Switzerland. Wait a minute! You said we're in Switzerland now. That's impossible, Isaac!"

"Nothing's impossible, Alicia. That carousel must have been some kind of time-travel machine. I don't understand it, but we're going to have to deal with it. For some reason, I think we're here to witness the martyrdom of Felix Manz."

"He was killed because he believed in adult baptism, and not infant baptism, right?" Alicia looked over at Isaac and then toward the tower in the middle of the river.

"Right. He told the government authorities that there was no evidence in the Bible for baptizing people before they were instructed about Christ. A person should *want* to be baptized, Manz told them."

"He wouldn't give up his beliefs, even though he knew it was dangerous," Alicia added. "He followed Jesus the way the Bible talks about. And then he started sharing with others what he'd learned. That's why the authorities killed him."

"You remember a lot from newcomers' class." Isaac smiled at Alicia. "I'm impressed."

"You should be. I'm trying to learn all I can. I believe the same things you do, and I want to follow Jesus the Mennonite way."

"Which is how?" Isaac asked in his best professor voice.

"By following the way of peace Jesus showed us." By listening to the Bible . . ."

Loud voices coming from near the tower interrupted their conversation.

A stout man with a black, plumed hat and black robe read from a scroll in his hands. "On this fifth day of the month of January in the year of our Lord, 1527, Felix Manz has been sentenced to die by the act of drowning. He has repeatedly broken the law by preaching and baptizing as if he were a priest in our state church."

"Aye, aye, drown him! He's a heretic!" shouted the crowd of men and women on the banks of the river. "He preaches against baptizing infants! He deserves to die!"

Alicia saw parents in the angry crowd lift toddlers onto their shoulders. "Do they really want their children to see what's going on?" she asked Isaac.

Isaac's dark brown eyes looked moist. He lowered his head. "Forgive them, God. They don't know what they're doing. Help me not to hate them."

"Isaac, look!" Alicia pointed toward the stone tower. "Is that Felix Manz?"

Guards stood on each side of a tall, thin man whose head was bowed, his hands tied in front of him. The man wore a green, long-sleeved shirt, and a small hat.

"They're leading Felix Manz out of the prison," Isaac whispered.

Three guards led Manz to what looked like a fish market by the river. A large sign with a fish was posted outside the small building.

"Listen. It sounds like someone's singing." Alicia strained to hear. "It's Felix Manz. He's singing! Does he know what they're going to do to him?"

"He knows, all right. He'll probably keep singing and preaching until they throw him in the river. He's a brave man, that's for sure."

"Isaac, why don't we stop his murder right now and change the course of history? Felix Manz doesn't have to die. We can rescue him. Maybe that's why we're here."

"No, we can't do that. We can't change what's happened in the past, Alicia. I wish we could. Boy, I'd make lots of changes—no wars, no killings, no famines, no hunger."

"I just feel so helpless." Alicia gripped the bare tree branch she had used to clear the ground. "One day people will realize that Felix Manz is right. People should be able to make up their own minds whether they want to follow Jesus or not. They can't make up their minds when they're still babies."

"He paid a terrible price for what he believed," Isaac said, looking straight ahead.

Alicia and Isaac lay on the frozen ground with their heads raised—watching, listening, and waiting until Alicia's lips were blue from the cold. The sun's rays didn't feel as warm as before.

They watched as Manz was forced into a boat with the guards, an executioner, and a pastor. The boat made its way toward a small fishing hut in the middle of the icy Limmat River.

"Believers baptism is the true baptism, according to the Word of God and the teachings of Christ. Praise God! Praise God, from whom all blessings flow!" Manz's voice was loud and strong as he preached to the onlookers from the boat.

A woman's voice called out from the shore, "Stand firm, Felix, stand firm."

A man's voice joined in, "Stand firm and suffer for Jesus' sake."

"I think that was his mother and brother," Isaac said softly.

The executioner in the boat pulled Felix Manz to his feet and lifted him up to the platform of the fishing hut. He shackled Manz's hands while he was seated, pulled them over his knees, and put a stick under his knees and over his arms. Alicia's knuckles turned white as she tightened her hands around the tree branch she was holding.

Manz sang in a loud voice, "*Domine in Manus tuas commendo spiritum meum.*"

"What's he singing?" Alicia asked.

"It's Latin for 'Lord, into your hands I commend my spirit.' "

Alicia looked back to see the executioner attach ropes to Manz's body and pull him off the platform. "No!" she cried out. Alicia could see Manz's head sinking beneath the icy water. "Help him!" she screamed. She scrambled to her feet and started to run for the river.

Isaac jerked himself up and ran after Alicia, tackling her just before she reached the river's edge. They could hear the sobs of Manz's mother and brother from the other side of the shore. Alicia's body shivered uncontrollably and her lips trembled as she tasted a flood of salty tears. Isaac's lips trembled too, but he stared straight ahead toward the river, keeping his eyes on the spot where he saw Felix Manz drown.

"How could people torture someone with such a horrible death? Never again, never again," he whispered to Alicia, not knowing how or when he'd be able to fulfill such a promise.

9

The Child and the Vine

Alicia and Isaac felt something warm and woolen fall across their backs. A small child stood looking down on them. Dressed in a dark brown, long dress and matching hood, she went first to Alicia and patted her on her back, as if soothing a crying baby. Then she looked at Isaac, smiled, and patted him on the head.

The child had covered them with her blanket and was about to hand them tiny pieces of a hard roll when a voice rang out from farther down the river bank. "Mary! Where are you? Come here at once!" The child turned and ran.

Exhausted with emotion, Alicia and Isaac fell into a deep sleep beneath the warm, comforting blanket. Who can say how long they slept on the banks of the Limmat River? They would have remained there much longer, except for a persistent tickle, the kind that makes your nose itch until you finally have to sneeze.

"*Achoo! Achoo!*" Isaac and Alicia sneezed in unison and jerked awake to a strange and stunning sight.

"What in the world? Isaac, we're covered in vines!"

"Tell me about it. How long have we been asleep?"

"Do you hear voices?" asked Alicia. "It sounds like someone's calling our names."

"Sh-h-h. I think I hear it. It sounds like someone's yelling from deep in a tunnel, or has a bad cell phone connection."

"Alicia, Isaac, can you hear me now? Where are you? Come back. Follow the vine, follow the vine."

"That sounds like Justin!" Alicia struggled to untangle vines from her ankles. A lone honey bee emerged from one of the vine's white, trumpet-shaped blossoms. The two watched the bee as it zoomed past their heads.

"We can probably thank Anna Bee for the experience we just encountered," Isaac said. "We were trying to find her when all of this strangeness happened, you know."

"Don't remind me. Let's just get out of here and find Justin and the others, Anna Bee or no Anna Bee. 'Follow the vine,' the voice said."

Isaac turned to Alicia. "Remember the vine lesson from the Bible? Jesus said he is the vine and we are the branches, and apart from him we can do nothing. Maybe we're living that lesson right now."

"How many stories and lessons can we be part of at one time?" Alicia frowned. "Anabaptist martyrs, the vine story in the Bible. Are we in the Twilight Zone or something?"

"You do know 'The Twilight Zone' was an old TV show, don't you?"

"Oh brother, don't tell me. Either I'm dreaming or my science teacher has a lot of explaining to do when I get back to school."

"Just study your quantum physics next year, my dear. And tell Professor Ballos that Isaac sent you."

"Yeah, right. I'm sure Mr. Ballos will be impressed with an eighth-grade geek's recommendation for his class."

"You'd be surprised at how much clout I have with Professor Ballos, my dear."

Alicia stomped on Isaac's foot. "Every time you say 'dear' to me, I'm going to stomp harder."

"I see you haven't taken the nonviolent communications class," Isaac retorted. "Perhaps I could recommend you to Mrs. Landis, my dear . . . *oops*, I mean 'dude.' "

"Listen, Isaac, we have to stop fooling around and find Justin and the others. Take hold of this vine and follow it. I'll be right behind you, watching to make sure no more stories or lessons grab hold of you and take you off somewhere."

Isaac grabbed the vine and started walking. He turned his head halfway around and asked, "And what if some mysterious stories grab hold of you?"

"They won't. I'm too practical. I think you and Anna Bee live in la-la land, so you attract stuff like that. I'm taking charge, Mr. Quantum Physics-Preacher Man, and we're getting back to real time and real friends. Keep walking and stop talking."

Isaac rubbed his eyes and squinted to see better. "Hey, Licia, is that a fire up ahead?" He stopped, so

Alicia could move up beside him. They peered through the wall of dense foliage before them.

"I'm not sure," Alicia replied. "I don't think we're in Switzerland anymore, that's for sure. And we're not back at camp either."

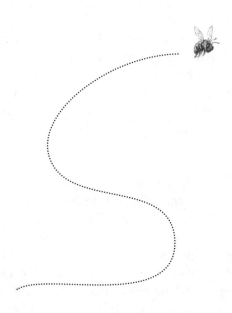

10

Fire and Ashes

By the time Isaac and Alicia reached the end of the vine, the fire Isaac had seen from a distance had died down. Before them were ashes and charred wooden stakes with chains hanging from them. Isaac felt a tugging on his pants leg. He looked down to find a little boy, about three years old, whimpering, and his face dirty with tears. The boy was strangely dressed, and looked like a picture Isaac had seen in a book.

"Isaac, we're in the middle of another story," Alicia whispered as she looked into the little boy's face. His sad, frightened eyes reminded her of Justin's the day he learned their mother had died. She turned away from the child. "Look, there's an older boy over there," she said. "He looks like he's out cold."

Isaac picked up the whimpering child. Alicia ran to help the other boy, who was lying flat on his back in the middle of a cobblestone street. Alicia thought he looked about 15 years old. The boy moaned and opened his eyes, looking up at Alicia. Then he looked past her and above her, as if seeing something else.

There was a loud sound above them, like a train speeding past on invisible rails. Alicia and the boy were blinded by a tremendous ball of red and yellow light that fell from nowhere.

Alicia held up her hands to shield herself from the intense light. Then she opened her eyes, but kept blinking, trying to adjust to the brightness. Several forms moved slowly through the sphere of light. They were headed toward them.

"We have to get out of here!" Alicia shouted to the boy. "Get up!" As Alicia reached down to help him, she heard a voice.

"Alicia! Alicia!"

Her heart felt like a rock, a pounding rock of fear. Then someone touched her, and she stumbled to the ground with the boy.

She looked up into the faces of Justin, Li, and Fabio.

"Licia, can you see me? Can you hear me?" Justin put his face close to hers.

"What in the world is going on?" Alicia spoke in rapid breaths. "Where did you and Fabio and Li come from? How did you get here?"

"Anna Bee's with us, too," said Justin. "She's not invisible to you, is she?"

"No. Uh, yeah, I see Anna," Alicia stammered.

"I think I have it figured out," said Li, as she and Fabio helped Alicia and the unknown boy to their feet. "We're in the middle of stories, Anabaptist hero stories," she said, brushing dirt and bits of vine from her T-shirt. "I don't know how or why. But it has something to do with the vine. Ever since we walked over that vine-covered bridge, things have been really weird. Fabio and I met Michael and Margareta Sattler in Germany. It was 1527! And Justin and Anna said they traveled to a castle in the Netherlands."

"We were all back at camp on the wooden bridge," added Fabio. "Then Anna took off after some bees again and we tried to stop her, but it was too late. We got caught up in the vines, pulled up in a flash of light, and then dropped here. It's totally strange. Have you figured out where we are now?"

"I think it's Antwerp, Belgium, October 6, 1573," said Isaac, who had joined them, still holding the little boy in his arms.

"Hey, who's the weird-looking kid you're holding?" Anna asked.

"I think it's Hans Mattheus Wens, son of Maeyken Wens, an Anabaptist martyr from the 16th century. This little boy's mother was burned at the stake with her tongue screwed to the roof of her mouth so she couldn't speak of her faith."

"Gross!" Anna shook her head in disgust. "These ghost stories are so real. It's like we're in the middle of a horror movie. This is some camp!"

"Who's the kid standing beside Alicia?" Anna continued. "Don't tell me he's wearing capri pants and knee socks!" She scrunched up her face. "Somebody, please take the dude shopping!"

"That's Adriaen Wens," Isaac answered, "Hans' brother. According to the story in *Martyrs Mirror*, Adriaen couldn't stay away from his mother's execution. He was scared, but he had to be with her one last time. He saw awful things—sheriff's men leading four prisoners, including his mother, to wooden stakes. Blood running from his mother's mouth and down her neck, onto her dress. A chain passed around her body and through a hole in the stake. He saw them set fire to the stake, and watched the flames surrounding his mother. That's when he fainted."

"No kidding! I would've fainted too," Anna declared.

"Thank you for your kindness." Adriaen spoke as Fabio stooped to pick up the boy's hat and hand it to him. "You are from a foreign country, that I can see from the way you are dressed. And your speech has an unfamiliar accent. Have you also been tortured for your obedience to Christ?" He looked at Anna and pointed to the black wires protruding from her ears down to a contraption around her neck.

"No, dude, this ain't torture. Want to listen to some fab music?" Anna held out her iPod's ear buds to Adriaen.

"I am sorry. I do not understand your ways," Adriaen replied. "But I thank you for remaining here with my brother Hans and me. Did you see the executions?" Before anyone could answer, he buried his head in one arm and with the other he hugged his chest tightly and rocked back and forth.

Alicia wanted to run away. She took a step backward and almost tripped over one of the street's uneven cobblestones. After what seemed like several minutes, the boy raised his head.

"My heart is breaking," he said, with tears streaming down his face. "My mother was in prison for six months. I could not see her or talk to her. But she sent me letters." He reached into his coat pocket, pulled out some pieces of paper, and carefully unfolded one of them.

"Oh, my dear son," he read, his voice cracking. "Though I will soon be taken from you, begin now in your youth to fear God. Then you shall have your mother again in the New Jerusalem, where we will never have to part again. My dear son, I hope now to go before you . . ."

Justin looked up at Adriaen and the others. "Where is 'New Jerusalem?'" he asked.

"It means 'heaven.'" Isaac answered. Adriaen nodded in agreement.

"That's where my mom is, too," Justin said. "I wonder if your mom has met my mom there." Before Adriaen could respond, Justin asked another question, "Why does your mom want you to be afraid of God?"

"Justin," Alicia broke in, "those are good questions, but I don't think Adriaen feels much like answering them right now."

Isaac spoke up, "People sometimes say 'fear God' to mean 'have great respect for God, because God is awesome.'"

"That sounds better," Justin said. "I'll try not to ask any more questions. Sorry, Adriaen."

Adriaen continued reading from the letter. "I commend you now to the Lord. May he keep you. I trust the Lord that he will do it, if you seek him. Love one another all the days of your life. Take little Hans in your arms now and then for me."

Justin looked at Hans, still snuggled in Isaac's arms and smiled. "We're already doing that for your mom," he said to Adriaen.

Adriaen read on. "My dear son, do not be afraid of this suffering. It is nothing compared to the suffering which endures forever. The Lord has taken away all my fear. I cannot fully thank my God for the grace which he has shown me. Goodbye once more, my dear son, Adriaen. I have written this after I was sentenced to die for the testimony of Jesus Christ, on the fifth day of October, in the year of our Lord Jesus Christ, 1573. Maeyken Wens."

Adriaen's voice broke as he finished, and he shut his eyes and bowed his head. Everyone was quiet.

"Your mom had a pretty name," said Justin, finally. "My mom's name was Adina Mae, Adina Mae Aduma. I think our moms would have liked each other."

"Thank you for listening to my mother's letter. It comforts me now, and I will always cherish her beautiful words." Adriaen smiled sadly and swallowed hard.

"Your mom was one brave woman," Anna pronounced. She took a bottle of water from her backpack, unscrewed the cap, and handed it to Adriaen. "Here, drink this. It will help your throat."

Adriaen took the water and gave some to Hans first. After drinking himself, he thanked Anna for her thoughtfulness. "Why was your mom in prison?" she asked. "My mom's in prison, too," she added, mumbling the words.

"My mother chose to obey the word of God, rather than follow the ways of the world," Adriaen replied. "She and Papa believed in reading God's word for themselves. She insisted on doing what the Bible said, even if it was against traditions and made the authorities angry. And so she was tortured, sentenced to death, and burned at the stake."

Straightening his weary body, Adriaen reached over to take his brother from Isaac's arms. "Thank you for comforting Hans."

51

Adriaen held his stomach as he stared at the charred stakes. He gently placed Hans on the ground and took hold of his small hand. They walked slowly toward the ash-covered ground and the four stakes, ugly and stark in the bright October sunshine. Alicia, Isaac, Li, Fabio, and Justin followed. Anna hesitated, then joined the others as they walked a few steps behind Adriaen and Hans.

Adriaen looked at the stake where his mother had died. Picking up a stick, he began poking through the ashes. Suddenly he bent down and picked up an object on the end of the stick. It was the tongue screw that had held his mother's tongue, so she could not speak in her last moments. Adriaen took out his handkerchief and carefully wrapped it up.

"Mama," he whispered. "I want you to know, I, too, will fear God and follow God's word with my whole heart. You have shown me the way."

Anna tried to find something to brush away the tears trickling down her face. The others were crying, too, but Anna didn't notice. She was thinking of her mother and how much she missed her, how much she loved her.

Suddenly she stepped forward and reached for Adriaen's hand. "I'm so sorry your mother had to die," she said softly.

Alicia moved forward next and took hold of Anna's hand. Isaac followed, taking Alicia's hand. Then Fabio and Li joined the circle. Hans was next. Justin stepped up, took the boy's tiny hand in his and folded his other hand around Adriaen's. The eight of them stood there silently, in the middle of a thousand ashes, the smell of burnt wood and flesh all around them.

Isaac began to sing, timidly at first and then louder and louder. Little Hans looked up at him. Anna and Adriaen joined their voices with the others as they picked up the words and the tune.

We are pilgrims on a journey,
we are trav'lers on the road.
We are here to help each other
walk the mile and bear the load.

I will hold the Christ light for you
in the night-time of your fear,
I will hold my hand out to you,
speak the peace you long to hear.

"Thank you, friends," Adriaen turned toward each one in the circle, his eyes steady. "May God be praised. I pray that you will take the fire of Christ's love from this place and leave the ashes of hate and violence behind."

Adriaen put the handkerchief with its precious token, his mother's tongue screw, into his pocket. His other pocket held his mother's letters. Taking little Hans by the hand, he turned toward home.

11

Camp Glow

Boy, you look like two tired puppies tonight," said Alicia and Justin's dad in his deep, baritone voice. "But there's a glow about you, too. Camp Amani Ya Juu must have been a good experience."

"Dad, your face looks a lot better." Alicia rested the cheese grater on the edge of her bowl and looked at his still-swollen lips. "How are you feeling?"

"I'm doing better all the time, Alicia."

Justin twisted his mouth back and forth. "We learned a lot about Anabaptist heroes today, Dad. It was so real, the things we saw and did. It was like we were really there."

"That's good, son. When history comes alive for you, it reaches not only your mind, but also your heart."

"It reached my heart all right. Standing there in that circle with little Hans and Adriaen—I felt so sad for them. I cried for their mom and my mom too."

Alicia saw Dad turn toward Justin with a quizzical look, but he didn't ask any questions. She was glad. How could they possibly explain what had happened to them and their friends without sounding like they'd totally lost their minds?

"And how did things go with Anna Bee?" Dad asked. "Did you help her feel at home? You know, it's hard to be a newcomer in a group."

"Dad, she's so cool," Justin piped up. "She knows a lot about nature, and she doesn't treat me like a kid."

Dad smiled and then glanced over at Alicia. "Have you been able to find any common interests with Anna?"

"Not really, Dad. We didn't have much time to talk today."

"Nope, that's for sure. We were like Peter Pan and Wendy," Justin said. "Flying into adventures, finding lost boys, zooming here and there. Dad, what do you know about Anabaptist martyrs? And can people go back in time . . ."

Alicia interrupted. "Justin, why don't you set the table in the dining room, and Dad and I can finish making the pizza?"

"Okay. Add lots of extra cheese, please. And don't take off on any vines till I get back." Justin flashed a big smile.

"Peter Pan and Wendy, taking off on vines?" Dad looked puzzled again. "Am I missing something?"

"Um-mm . . ." Alicia stammered, "I think Justin is talking about the vine lesson Isaac shared with us today. Isaac knows a lot about the Bible, and he wants to be a preacher."

"I've been impressed with Isaac's knowledge of the

Bible," Dad agreed. "He has a love for God's word. He'll make a fine preacher. By the way, we got some mail today from your school—a list of choices for next year's special classes. 'The Bible and You' is one of them. I'd like you to consider taking that, Alicia."

"Was quantum physics listed too, Dad?"

"Well, let's take a look. Here's the list."

Alicia wiped her hands on a towel and reached for the sheet of paper. She ran her finger down the page. "Introduction to Quantum Physics, Mr. Ballos," she read. "That and the Bible class—those are the ones I want to take, Dad."

During supper, Justin told them all sorts of honey bee facts. "You were right, Dad. Anna Bee really is a bee expert. Did you know that one hive can hold up to 80,000 bees? And a queen bee can lay up to 3,000 eggs in one day? I asked Anna lots of bee questions. Every time she saw a bee today, she told me something else. Her dad has a honey business, and Anna helps him. They used to send her mom jars of honey to share with the other soldiers. But they can't send her anything where she is now."

Dad nodded. "I'm glad you're getting to know Anna better. You saw bees today, eh?" his swollen eyebrows lifted a bit.

"Just a few. Anna said they were probably from her dad's bee hives. She's going to count the bees she sees at camp this week. Dad, can you get us up earlier in the morning? Anna, Fabio, Isaac, and Li are coming at seven o'clock. We're going to talk about what we did at camp today."

"Be glad to, son. I'm really glad you and your sister are so excited about camp. I'll have to commend the camp counselors when I see them later this week."

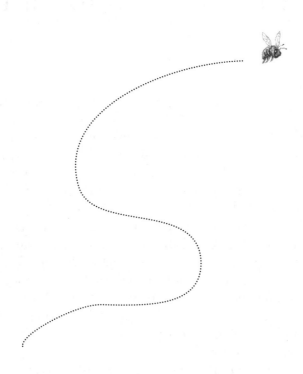

12

From Carousel to Castle

Alicia was bone tired, but she knew she had to find out where Justin had been earlier that day. They'd been separated for more than two hours. Had he been to Switzerland and back, too? Had he seen Feliz Manz drown in the Limmat River?

It was too mind-boggling to think about for long. Alicia's head was full of questions and fears and wonder. A headache had lodged itself right behind her eyes. Maybe her talk with Justin would have to wait until morning. She walked to his room to say goodnight.

Justin had pulled the bed sheet over his head, and a yellow glow shone through the fabric. *He must be reading with a flashlight again,* Alicia thought. She smiled and called from the doorway, "Sleep tight and don't let the bugs bite."

Justin's head popped out from the covers. "Hey, sis, wanna see what Anna Bee's cell phone recorded today?" His eyes were as big as whoopie pies. "We were there, Anna and me, but I still can't believe it."

"You were where?" Alicia hurried into the room and sat down on the edge of the bed. "I want to know everything you did today and every place you went."

"Licia, we talked to a boy before he was murdered." Justin's voice was solemn.

"*Murdered!*"

"We were in another time zone. We were in the Netherlands, and it was 1550."

"1550? The Netherlands?"

"Yeah, that's what I said. When we got off the carousel, we were in a beautiful forest with the tallest trees I've ever seen. We walked along a path to a clearing, and came on an awesome castle. Look, here's a picture Anna took."

"The castle at Leeuwarden?" Alicia recognized it from a book.

"How'd you know that?"

"Mrs. Krehbiel's Anabaptist History class."

"Anna and I were there, talking to Jacques Dosie, but he wasn't history. He was real," said Justin.

"Tell me everything," Alicia urged.

"When we walked up to the castle, the guards tried to shoo us away. They called us 'shabby urchins from the forest.'"

"Did they try to hurt you?" Alicia frowned.

"No. When the owners of the castle, Lord and Lady Friesland, saw us, they thought we were beggars. I guess the lady felt sorry for us, 'cause she invited us inside for a meal. She even gave us some clothes to put on, because we were dressed so 'pitifully.' I videoed the part after the guards brought in Jacques Dosie." Justin handed her the cell phone.

"Didn't they wonder what you were doing?"

Justin smiled. "Nope. I'm a good spy. The long sleeve of the fancy shirt Lady Friesland gave me covered the phone, and no one was looking at me anymore. They were all looking at the lord and lady and Jacques Dosie."

Justin and Alicia watched the video, their heads close together. Alicia's eyes widened as she took in the strange images and voices coming from the small screen.

"This is the fancy room where they took us, and that's Lady and Lord Friesland." Justin pointed.

"Sh-h-h, be quiet, so I can hear what they're saying," Alicia whispered.

"What do you say, my lord?" The lady was speaking, her hand on her husband's arm. "I should like to hear this lad, Jacques Dosie's, story."

"My dear, I too am curious," the man replied.

"Isn't it strange that one so young should be accused of heresy?" the lady asked.

The man motioned to a guard hovering nearby. "Summon the lad, Jacques Dosie, from the prison. We wish to examine him."

Justin stopped the video. "We waited about an hour before the boy showed up. Anna thought we were in a history reenactment, like at a museum, so she got right into it. Did you know she brought a microphone to camp?"

"No, you're kidding," Alicia groaned. "Don't tell me she started rapping at the castle!"

"No, but she pretended to be a reporter with the

microphone in her hand. She asked one of the servant girls a question. I'm pretty sure the girl thought the microphone was a weapon, because she fainted. It caused a big commotion."

"It's a wonder they didn't lock Anna up." Alicia shook her head.

"One of the guards wanted to, but Lady Friesland stopped him. I think she liked us. I bet she would have adopted us if we hadn't zoomed back to camp."

Alicia rolled her eyes. "Can I see the rest of the video, please?"

Justin pressed the button on the cell phone, and Alicia saw a boy in shabby clothes standing between two guards in the doorway.

"Come with me," Lady Friesland said to him. Together they walked over to her husband.

"Ah, so this is the lad," he said. The boy held his head high and his shoulders straight, as if he weren't afraid at all.

"What is your name?"

"Jacques Dosie, my lord."

"How old are you?"

"Fifteen years, my lord."

"Why is it you are in prison? They say you are guilty of heresy."

"Hold it!" Alicia whispered. "How did you get so close to them? I can see the boy's eyes glistening!"

"I kept low and moved in between all the people, till I got as close as I could. Everyone was watching the lord and lady with Jacques Dosie, so they didn't pay any attention to me."

61

"You were brave."

Justin turned the video back on. Jacques was standing even taller, his eyes wide and bright as he spoke.

"I am in prison only because I believe in Christ and will never forsake him."

Lord Friesland raised his eyebrows and began to ask another question, but one of his advisers interrupted him and took him aside. Coming back, he said, "My dear, I am sorry, but I must leave. The archduke is here for his appointment."

He laid his hand gently on Jacques' shoulder. "Son, please mend the error of your ways. I take no pleasure seeing you deprived of your freedom."

He left, and the lady motioned to Jacques. "Come, let us sit down. I would like to talk to you further."

She led him to two purple velvet chairs by a window with dark green drapery. They sat facing each other.

"Jacques," questioned the lady, "do you belong to the people who rebaptize? The ones who are creating rebellion in our country?"

Several of the nobles and ladies in the room moved closer to listen.

"My lady, I don't know any rebellious people," Jacques answered. "We would much rather help our enemies, giving them food and drink if they are hungry or thirsty. We do not resist them with either revenge or violence."

One of the nobles snorted. "Ha, it would be a different story if you had the power to do otherwise."

"Oh, no," protested Jacques. "We believe it is wrong to resist the authorities with swords and violence. We would rather suffer persecution and death."

He sighed. "My lady, people use rumors as reason to persecute us. But we must endure patiently."

Lady Friesland looked down at her hands and twisted one of her rings. "Jacques, do you believe everyone is wrong who is not baptized according to your way?"

"No, my lady. Judging who is right and who is wrong belongs to God alone. Baptism is merely a sign of obedience to God."

"What about *infant* baptism?" someone in the room asked.

Jacques turned and answered, "It is not a command of God, but an invention of people. Infants do not know what is required in baptism. Christ has promised them the kingdom of God through grace."

Lady Friesland looked angry. She stood up and spoke harshly to Jacques. "I consider this the worst thing you have said, that you do not believe children should be baptized. All Germany—in fact, every kingdom—practices this."

Jacques nodded solemnly. "We are despised everywhere because of our beliefs."

The lady's face softened, and she took one of Jacques' hands in her own. "My dear son, I beg you to change your mind and get out of this trouble. I myself will arrange for your release."

"Thank you, my lady, for your affection," Jacques replied, "but I will not change my faith to please you or any other person, unless you can prove to me with scriptures that I am wrong. I have given myself entirely to God, whether I live or die."

The two were silent for a time, their faces sad. "My son," the lady pleaded, "I beg you to repent of your baptism. You are so young. If you should die for this hopeless cause, it would be a heavy cross for my heart."

"My lady, I cannot see what crime I have committed," the boy replied. "It is not my own way I follow, but the way taught by Jesus Christ."

The lady rose from her chair. Jacques also stood and bowed his head respectfully. A guard quickly took him from the room.

Justin stopped the video and looked at Alicia. "The next part shows Anna talking to Jacques. We followed him and the guard to the jail cell in the castle, and sneaked into the cell before the door was closed."

Alicia looked alarmed. "You were locked up in a cell with Jacques Dosie?"

"Yes. We knew the guards were going to take him back to the main prison soon, and we had to talk to him ourselves. Anna wanted to help him escape."

"Help him escape! You could've been killed!"

"We didn't think about that. We just wanted to help him." Justin pushed the button again.

Jacques Dosie sat at a heavy table, his arms and legs shackled to a bench. Across from him was Anna, a velvet cape around her shoulders.

"Justin and I will help you escape," she whispered.

"When the guard opens the door, here's what we'll do . . ."

"No, my lady. You are kind, but I cannot run away. I am willing to die for Christ. Besides, it would cause the guards trouble if I escaped. They might be severely punished or even put to death."

"Better them than you!" said Anna.

"No, my lady. I am willing to give my life for what I believe. But I cannot cause other people to die because of me.

"Please return to your land," he added, "and tell the story of those who are being killed for their faith."

Alicia heard Justin speak. "We can teach your stories in our history classes," he said. "And write them in books."

"We can make movies and DVDs," Anna added.

"I do not understand," Jacques said, "but thank you for staying here with me until the guards return. My new friends, I urge you to live for Christ."

The screen went blank and Justin looked at Alicia. "That's where we were today. Anna thinks we were in some kind of history museum with actors, but I think it was for real."

Alicia nodded, "I think it was real too, Justin."

13

Chasing Bees Again

The next morning, when Dad went to wake Justin and Alicia, he was surprised to see they were already dressed. "Wow, this is the earliest I've seen you two up in a long time. I'll have to learn Camp Amani Ya Juu's secret. Whatever they're doing must be pretty exciting!"

"That's for sure," Justin said. "I can't wait for today's adventures. I'm ready to meet some more heroes. And who knows where we'll go to find them? Could be Africa, could be China, could be . . ."

"Justin," Alicia interrupted, "we'd better get our breakfast bars and see if Li, Fabio, and Isaac are waiting for us." She wasn't sure how much they should tell Dad about the strange happenings at camp, especially across the vine-covered bridge.

"Don't forget Anna Bee. I'm sure she'll be with us too. She had a blast yesterday."

"Right, how could I ever forget Anna Bee?" Alicia lowered her voice to add, "I might want to try, but I think it's too late for that."

As they walked to camp, the Menno Fab Five

talked about all that had happened to them the day before. Anna rode beside them on her bike, circling around every few feet to keep from getting ahead. They were still sharing stories when they got to camp.

"Welcome back to Camp Amani Ya Juu, happy campers!" the counselors greeted them. This time the quilts on the lawn were all touching each other.

"Do you notice something different today?" asked Christina as the kids scrambled to find places to sit.

"The quilts are one big block of color," Li said. "They look like they're all one piece, instead of separate quilts."

"That's right," said Tim, the tallest counselor. "We want you to start thinking of yourselves as one unit, not as separate quilts or individual planets, millions of light-years from each other. Can you think of other things that need each other?"

"You bet I can!" Anna threw up her right arm with her finger pointing skyward, cocked her head, and swayed back and forth. "Bees, bees, bees! The queen needs the workers, the workers need the queen, it's all pretty special, when you know just what it means."

"I told you she looked like a rapper." Alicia rolled her eyes. "At least she didn't rap at the castle."

"What castle?" Isaac jerked his head toward Alicia. "What planet are you on this morning?"

"I'll clue you in later. It's beyond belief, that's all I can say. I'm just glad Anna didn't wear that bomber T-shirt again. I can't even imagine what Jacques Dosie thought of that."

"Jacques Dosie? You mean the one we studied about in Anabaptist History class? He probably wouldn't know what it was . . . Hey, wait a minute! Are you telling me you talked to Jacques Dosie?" Isaac's eyes grew wider.

"No, *I* didn't talk to him, but Anna did."

"*Anna?* How can that be? She's barely learned how to say 'Anabaptist' instead of 'anti-baptist,' and our faith heroes are already welcoming her into the fold?" Isaac squinted his eyes and looked serious. "You know what? I think it's a good thing."

"Sometimes I just can't figure you out, Isaac Thomas Roth," Alicia sighed. "You actually want to invite people like Bee-Girl into our church group?"

"Mark my words, dear . . . I mean, Alicia, people like Anna Bee help us see things with fresh eyes—fresh as honey from a bee."

"Oh, brother, spare me your philosophies. It's too early for that. Justin and I stayed up late watching Anna's video of Jacques Dosie. Maybe you can watch it later. I still don't get what's going on."

"Hey, Alicia! Isaac!" Li and Fabio motioned to get their attention. "Come on. Tim says we can choose between two activities this morning—planting a peace garden or making a peace feast."

"I know what I'm choosing," Justin said, smiling. "Peace feast! That means food, right?"

"If we go to the garden plot," Li said, "we'll pass by the vine bridge. We could meet at the bridge for a minute and still get to the garden on time. We can make a peace feast later."

She looked at her watch. "It's 9:20 now. We need to be at the garden by 9:30."

Isaac and Alicia didn't hesitate. They'd already planned to visit the bridge sometime that morning.

"That's my vote," said Alicia.

"Mine too," said Isaac.

"Count me in," added Fabio.

"Hey, where's Anna?" Justin looked all around.

"Did you really think she'd stick beside us today?" Alicia shook her head. "She's probably off chasing bees."

"Well, I'll chase bees, too, then," said Justin, running toward the bridge.

The others gathered their backpacks and took off after Justin. They stopped suddenly when they saw the bridge. The vines were gone.

"What in the world? This *is* the same bridge, isn't it? Or are we lost?" Alicia glanced at the others, who looked as dumbfounded as she felt.

"Maybe the vines were there to help us go where we needed to yesterday," Isaac guessed. "Maybe we don't need them today."

Li spotted Anna on the other side of the bridge. "There are more stepping stones on the floor of the bridge," Anna yelled. "Look at them! They're cool. There's a new trail over here too."

Justin and Li led the way onto the bridge, hurrying toward Anna on the other side. Li looked down as one of the stones lit up in a soft glow. She gasped and knelt down to touch it. It was decorated with Chinese symbols and red flowers. In the center were five triangles, one square, and one parallelogram—all creating shapes of humans, buildings, and countries.

"What's that?" Isaac asked, kneeling beside Li.

Anna joined the group on the bridge, eager to see what they'd discovered. "Wow, that's awesome," she breathed, looking down at the glowing stone. "What does it mean?"

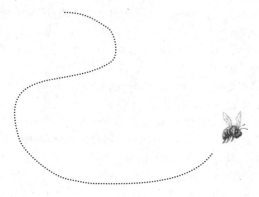

14

The Chinese Puzzle

It's a Chinese *tangram*, and it means we have a puzzle to solve," Li answered softly.

"Mennonites love puzzles," Isaac said. "This'll be fun. Can you help us solve it, Li?"

"See those three images?" Li asked, pointing to three of the triangles. "They represent Indonesia, Russia, and Vietnam. The human image there is Tee Siem Tat. I know his story."

"You do?" Alicia looked surprised.

"Tell us the story, Li," said Justin. "Is he an Anabaptist hero like the people we found yesterday?"

"Yes, at least he is to me," replied Li, almost in a whisper.

"I hope the story's easier to understand than his name," Anna declared. "Who ever heard of a name like that?"

"*My* name is like that," Li responded. "Li Pham Siem Tat."

"Oh, that's funny! Do kids tease you? It's kind of a weird name when you say it all together at one time.

'Lee' is okay, but I wouldn't go around telling people the whole thing," Anna advised.

"The nerve of . . ." Alicia started to speak.

"Anna, that's nice of you to think of ways to protect Li from bullies," broke in Justin. "You're right. I guess it's better to stay quiet if you don't want to cause trouble."

"You're related to the figure in the puzzle?" Fabio asked Li.

"Yes."

"Go on, tell us the story of the figure, Li," Fabio encouraged her.

"Okay, if you're interested in my ancestor hero, I will tell you his story. Please sit down next to the stone that glows."

Li smiled at the others as she began. "Many years ago, my great-grandfather, Tee Siem Tat, who lived in Java, became very ill."

"Where's Java?" interrupted Justin.

"It's an island of Indonesia. Great-Grandfather sent for doctor after doctor, but they could find nothing wrong with him.

"'But I am sick!' Great-Grandfather insisted. 'I feel terrible. Can you not help me?'

"'We are sorry. We cannot help you,' they told him.

"Meanwhile, my great-grandmother found a Bible and began to read it. Every time she came to verses that told of Jesus dying on the cross, she began to cry. Finally, Great-Grandmother and Great-Grandfather, who was still very sick, decided to visit the Salvation

Army center in Rembang, Indonesia. They wanted to find out more about the Bible and the Christian life. Great-Grandfather Tee noticed that he felt much better after the worship service there, and soon he was completely well!"

"I bet he just had bad allergies, and they gave him bee pollen and honey to eat," said Anna, with a smirk. "That's what I'd do."

Alicia scowled at her. "Li," she asked, "How did your great-grandfather *really* get well?"

"I don't know. But the story gets even better," she said with a twinkle in her eye. "Great-Grandfather and Great-Grandmother were so excited that they invited the Salvation Army to hold church services in their own home. One day, during a service, Great-Grandfather decided to follow Jesus and become a Christian, and Great-Grandmother did too."

"That was a miracle!" said Justin, "Just like your great-grandfather's healing."

"God at work through the Holy Spirit," said Isaac.

"Don't start with the spooky spirit talk, you guys," Alicia said, rolling her eyes.

"That's not the end of the story," continued Li. "Great-Grandfather wanted to find out what other Christians believed, so he visited many churches and missionaries. He believed the teaching of a Mennonite missionary, Johann Thiessen from Russia, was closest to what the Bible said. And so he became a Mennonite.

"Missionary Thiessen baptized him on December 6,

1920, along with Great-Grandmother and 24 others." Li looked down at the stone again and touched her great-grandfather's figure. "Father says Great-Grandfather and Great-Grandmother's decision to become Mennonite Christians was the beginning of our family's walk in the footsteps of Jesus."

"I'm going to be baptized one day," Justin said. "Dad says baptism is a sign that we've decided to follow Jesus. I guess I could be baptized right now, then." He smiled at the others.

"Well, what are we waiting for?" shouted Isaac and Fabio. "Let's take him to the creek!"

Picking up Justin by the hands and feet and swinging him between them, the two boys headed for the water below the bridge.

"Hey, wait a minute!" Justin yelled, trying to twist free. "You have to be a preacher to baptize me!"

"Well, I'm planning to be a preacher," Isaac laughed as they got closer to the water. "And I already know the words to say."

"Yeah, we'll just throw you in, and Isaac can say a few words as you sink to the bottom and float to the top," Fabio teased.

Suddenly Anna ran up beside Fabio and threw her full weight into his shoulder, knocking him to the ground. He let go of Justin's feet as he was falling, throwing Isaac off balance. Anna rammed into Isaac too, sending him sprawling to the ground.

"You're not doing anything to Justin!" she spat out. "What if he can't swim? Are you crazy?"

"Cool down, Bee-Girl." Alicia ran up beside them.

"Justin's a great swimmer. But I agree with you, they don't need to throw him in the creek." She glared down at Fabio and Isaac.

"Okay, sorry. We didn't realize you couldn't take a joke." Isaac stood up, then turned to Justin. "Sorry, bro. No harm done?"

"No harm done," Justin agreed, giving Isaac their special high-five.

"I'm sorry, too," added Fabio, and held out his hand to Justin.

Li, still on the bridge, yelled to them. "Hey, macho boys who try to throw small boy into creek, please come back and help me with this puzzle!" She was studying the other figures on the stone.

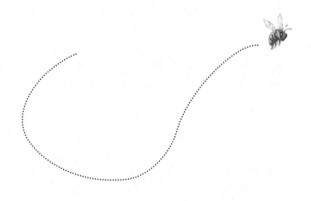

15

A Football and a Dove

Anna outran the others back to the bridge. "What does this look like?" Li asked her, pointing to the stone.

"Looks like a football to me," Anna answered.

"Isn't that a dove next to it?"

"Maybe. Some kind of bird, anyway. And the bird and football are beneath the triangle you said shows the outline of Vietnam."

"That's right." Li nodded. "A football, a dove, and the country of Vietnam. They have to be connected somehow."

"Weird. What does a football have to do with a bird and Vietnam?" Anna crinkled up her forehead in thought.

Alicia hurried up, followed by Justin, Isaac, and Fabio. She looked intently at the stone's markings. "I know the answer to this part of the puzzle."

"You do?" the others asked in unison.

"Sure. Why are you so surprised?"

"Well, let's just say you haven't shown much interest in Mennonite puzzle-solving to date," said Isaac.

"She showed interest last night in Anna's cell-phone video of Jacques Dosie," Justin put in. "And that's a puzzle, 'cause it's history and real at the same time."

"Anna has a video of Jacques Dosie?" Li and Fabio looked at Anna and then at the others. "Did you get it from the counselors?"

"No, I didn't get it from anyone," Anna said. "Justin took the video on my cell phone."

"Who played the part of Jacques? Was this for a special class or something?" asked Li.

"No, some other kid played the part of Jacques. I didn't know him. But the castle was awesome."

"Sounds like we missed a fun camp activity yesterday, Li, but I guess we can watch the video later," Fabio said.

"Let's all watch it together." Alicia turned toward the others. "I'd like to see it again. Maybe together we can solve the puzzles and muddles we're running into this week."

"Muddles? What're those?" asked Justin.

"Sorry, *muddle* means 'state of mental confusion.' "

"Oh, yeah, you can say that again." Justin grinned.

"Okay, you five Mennos," Alicia said, including Anna without thinking, "listen up. Here's the answer to the puzzle.

"The three symbols—the football, the dove, and Vietnam—point to one important Anabaptist hero. Remember our Peace Heroes class last year?"

"Tell us, more, dear . . . uh, I mean, Alicia, O Learned One," Isaac said.

"Yeah, that class was a long time ago. Maybe we were at choir practice or something," put in Fabio. "Or maybe you have a better memory."

Alicia gave a big sigh. "All right, you guys, since obviously none of you were paying attention in class, I'll tell you the whole story."

"I wasn't even *living* here," interrupted Anna, "so I *couldn't* have taken the class."

"Please be seated and keep your mouths closed till I tell you the story." Alicia tried not to smile, but this was sort of fun.

"I can help," Li said. "I know the story."

"All right, Li, let's begin. You go first."

"Ted Studebaker was killed during the Vietnam War, when he was 25 years old," Li began softly. "He was a conscientious objector who refused to serve in the military."

"But he was willing to go to Vietnam and work as a volunteer with Vietnam Christian Service," Alicia added.

Anna yawned and fumbled through her backpack to find her iPod. She turned it on.

THIS IS ABC NEWS from New York. . . blasted the sound from the iPod. Anna's eyes got as big as pizzas. She'd never turned the volume that loud, and never recorded a newscast.

I'm Howard K. Smith with the Harry Reasoner Report, continued the voice, *and here's the news for Tuesday, May 4, 1971 . . .*

"Hey, that's an old recording. Where'd you get it?" asked Fabio.

"I . . . I don't know. I didn't put that on my iPod," said Anna, bewildered. Then she glared at them. "Hey, who's been messing with my stuff? And somebody's been messing with the volume, too! Nobody's supposed to hear it but me."

. . . When Ted Studebaker went to war, he took no weapons . . . The man's voice coming from the iPod got louder.

"Wait a minute—he said 'Ted Studebaker!' Did you hear that?" Isaac looked confused. "Are you sure you don't have a recording of a 1971 newscast?"

"Yeah, maybe the counselors gave you that, along with the Jacques Dosie video," Fabio added.

"Didn't you hear what I said before?" Anna glared at them. "Nobody gave me any video, and nobody gave me a recording from 1971! Do I look like I'd be interested in a newscast from 1971? I wasn't even born then. My *mom* probably wasn't born then. And we wouldn't want to listen to a crazy news recording about someone not wanting to go to war. My mom volunteered to *go* to war!"

The voice from Anna's iPod continued . . . *Ted took instead a guitar, a small tape recorder, and a dedication to the idea that more can be accomplished with tools than with guns . . .* Anna frantically tried to stop the voice from speaking. But the man's voice just got louder.

. . . Ted's assignment with the Vietnam Christian Service was to help the mountain people of the village of Di Linh. He worked there for two years and planned to stay a third. He fell in love with Ven Pak,

a gentle Chinese girl from Hong Kong. She also was a volunteer. They got married . . .

Anna gave up and began to listen. The others leaned toward her and the iPod in her hand, listening intently. Then they heard another voice.

My name is Phyllis Cribby. I was a nurse with the Vietnam Christian Service. At one o'clock a.m. on April 26, 1971, I was still upstairs in our house in Di Linh. Ted and Ven Pak were in their room downstairs. A few minutes after one o'clock, a rocket or mortar exploded in our back yard, very close to the house. This was followed by two or three more, each sounding closer and breaking some window glass. I ran downstairs, and Ted was in the hall calling Ven Pak . . .

Anna was listening as intently as the others now.

. . . All of us ran down the hall to the bunker. Suddenly Ted turned back and ran to his room, and just after that a charge went off by the back door. The noise and pressure from it were tremendous and we were momentarily stunned. We were afraid it might have killed Ted, but then we heard him whisper loudly, 'I'm okay!' Ven Pak and I and another volunteer crawled quickly into the bunker . . .

"What's a bunker?" Justin whispered.

"Sh-h-h, I'll tell you later," said Alicia.

. . . Immediately after that we heard some men entering the house. We could hear them walking around. Then we heard some talking in Ted's room, and we heard him say 'Khong co.' That means 'Not have.' There was a lot of noise and confusion, and I

heard two shots. We didn't hear Ted say anything else. Then someone came down the hall in our direction . . .

"Oh no! Please don't kill them!" cried Justin. Anna reached over and put her hand on his shoulder.

. . . I was near the door, and when the intruder opened it and shone the light in, he could see only me. I started to stand up, but he told me to get down. He closed the door and walked away . . .

Justin took a deep breath and relaxed his shoulders.

. . . We thought the men might have left mines or traps, so we waited for daylight to come out of our hiding place. I went down the hall to Ted's room. Things from the cupboards and shelves were scattered all over the room. I walked toward the closet. I could see legs near the closet door. I knew it was Ted. He was slumped against the wall of the closet, and there was a lot of blood around him. I knew he was dead . . .

Li and Alicia gasped. Justin bowed his head and put his hand to his mouth.

The voice from the iPod changed again. *Hello, my name is Ven Pak Studebaker, Ted's wife. We were married only a week before Ted was killed. Some of you don't know how much my life was changed since I have known him, especially how he helped me understand about true love and peace. I think I can continue to learn from Ted's influence and memory. His belief that love is stronger than hate was evident in the way he died. He was truly a man of peace, and he believed strongly in trying to follow the example of Jesus Christ as best as he knew how. I would like for you to hear a recording that Ted made while he was in Vietnam . . .*

One last voice rang out, deep, strong and confident. *My name is Ted Studebaker. . .*

Justin lifted his head and straightened his shoulders.

. . . Above all, Christ taught me to love all people, including enemies, to return good for evil, and that all men are brothers. I condemn all war and refuse to take part in it in any active or violent way. I believe love is a stronger and more enduring power than hatred for my fellow man, regardless of who they are or what they believe.

Anna's back stiffened, and her hand tightened painfully on Justin's shoulder. "What that man said makes me think of my mom. I'm afraid for her. She was stationed overseas with the military. They wanted her to get information from the prisoners, but she refused to torture them. That's what my dad told me. And now she's in prison, because she didn't obey her commander."

Alicia looked at Li, her eyebrows raised in double arches. Then she turned to Anna. "That's awful that they put your mom in prison for doing the right thing. Do you want to tell us more? Is there anything we can do to help?"

"No, I don't want to tell you more. There's nothin' anyone can do to help!" snapped Anna. "And don't ask me any more questions about it." She jumped up. "Hey, what did the football mean? No one explained the stupid football!"

"I can tell you about the football," said Alicia.

"Ted Studebaker loved playing football in high school. He even wrote an essay about it. So the football, the dove of peace, and the country of Vietnam all represent the story of Ted Studebaker. He's another Anabaptist hero."

Suddenly, the static from Anna's iPod was deafening. The strong and confident voice was back. *This is Ted Studebaker. Did someone mention football? . . .*

"Wow, what's going on?" Fabio asked.

"Like I said before, we're in the middle of a ghost story," Anna said.

. . . Playing football was a great experience for me in high school. I prayed to God to let me play, and did the best job I knew how . . .

Justin twisted his mouth back and forth. "I want to play football, and I want to teach peace," Justin declared. "With God's help, I'll do it." His voice sounded like Ted Studebaker's, strong and confident.

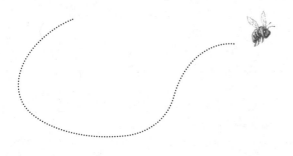

16

Hummingbird Time

"Oh no! What time is it? We've been here for hours, and we're supposed to be planting a peace garden!" Li looked at her watch. Then she shook her arm and tapped the watch with her finger. "I think my watch stopped. It says 9:23. That can't be right! Isaac, what time do you have?"

"Both our watches must've stopped. Mine says 9:23 too."

"Either that or we're in some kind of time warp," put in Fabio.

"Read the sky." Anna pointed to the east. "The sun's still in almost the same place as when we were sitting on the quilts. Maybe we're in hummingbird time. Native American legend says that hummingbirds float free of time."

"I think I like hummingbird time," said Justin.

"Something weird always happens around this bridge," Fabio said as he stepped from the bridge onto the grassy slope.

"Hummingbird time or not, we'd better get to the

garden," Alicia said. "If the watches are right, we still have seven minutes."

"And if the watches are wrong, we missed the peace garden activity," Justin said.

"But the peace feast might still have some food to share with time-lost nomads," Isaac pointed out.

"For sure." Justin smiled and gave Isaac a high-five.

"I think we could all use a little extra nourishment right about now," added Fabio.

The six campers—Alicia, Fabio, Li, Anna, Isaac, and Justin—half walked, half ran toward the garden plot Tim had pointed out earlier. They merged into the line of other campers on the same trail.

"I like trails," said Justin. "They lead you where you need to go."

"Depends if you take the right trail," Fabio added.

"All trails lead somewhere, and people usually find the one they need," Anna said. She stooped to look at a yellow-flowered fern. "That's different. I've never seen anything like it."

"Anna knows a lot about nature, guys." Justin looked at Anna and smiled.

"Back to the trail business, dear." Isaac reminded her.

"*What* did you call me?" Anna's eyes flashed. "If you want to keep your tacky khaki shoes clean, don't ever use that word again with me!" She stomped her shoe on his.

"Ouch! I think I've infiltrated the secret society of shoe-stompers. And you and Alicia are co-presidents.

Message received loud and clear, especially by my foot." Isaac grimaced as he rubbed the toe of his shoe.

"As I was saying," he began again. "Trails are a lot like roads. Don't you think you can take the wrong trail sometimes?"

"Sure," Anna said, "but if you read the markers along the way, you'll know you're on the wrong one."

"And then you have to decide whether or not to turn around." Li looked at Anna and smiled. She was starting to like Anna, even if she was different from anyone she'd ever met.

"I see we're almost at the end of the trail, Menno Fab Five." Isaac turned around and was surprised to see Alicia, Li, and Anna walking almost shoulder to shoulder.

"Taken a math class lately?" Alicia asked. "There are *six* of us, not five. Unless your quantum physics have reduced our mass by one whole person."

Just testing to see if you're listening," Isaac retorted with a laugh. "Of *course* there are six of us. The 'Slick Six' is our name, and we're ready for any game."

"Dude, make that the Menno Slix Sick," Justin added. "Whoops, that's hard to say!" He laughed. "Slick six, slick stix, stick slix . . . I give up!"

"Are we there yet?" Alicia groaned. "Please tell me we're there."

Just then they spotted the clearing for the garden plot.

"What time is it?" Alicia looked at Li and Isaac.

"Nine-thirty exactly," Isaac looked at his watch.

"Check! Nine-thirty here, too," said Li, holding out her watch.

"Then our bridge adventure really did last only three minutes?" Anna raised her eyebrows and looked at the others.

"Don't even try to figure it out," Isaac replied. "This will take some serious spy work."

"I want to spy, play football, and teach peace," Justin declared. "And eat!"

"You're going to have one weird career when you grow up, *hombrecito*," said Fabio.

"Hey, I'm no *hombrecito*. I'm a slick stick, remember?" Justin grinned and gave Fabio a high-five.

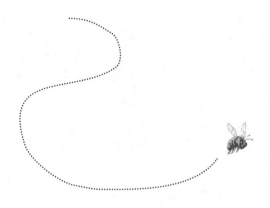

17

Clues in the Garden

Campers, please gather 'round in the circle," Christina called to the last of the kids arriving at the garden clearing. "Jesse and I are going to help you plant Camp Amani Ya Juu's first peace garden of the summer. The other counselors have asked us to plant some foods we can use for peace feasts. What do you recommend?"

The campers shouted suggestions.

"Strawberries for strawberry sundaes!"

"Potatoes for French fries!"

"Tomatoes for ketchup!"

"Watermelons for spitting seeds!"

Everyone laughed.

"How 'bout broccoli?" Jesse shouted.

"*No-o-o!*" the campers replied.

"Wait a minute! I *like* broccoli," Justin said. "Especially with lots of cheese on it."

"Is there any food you don't like, bro?" Fabio pretended to shovel food into his mouth.

"All right, campers, let's get to work." Jesse started handing out hoes to everyone. "While you're planting good things to share with others, you may find some hidden treasures. When you do, just yell, and we'll all come over and take a look. Okay?"

"What kinds of treasures?" asked one of the campers. "Chests full of chocolates?"

"Yeah, chocolate's good with cheese," Justin said.

"Nope, something better than that," replied Jesse. "Connections."

"Connections to our past," added Christina. "We can't understand the present unless we've learned from the past. And we can't plan the future unless we understand ourselves and our faith roots. So, you might say we're digging for roots."

"Sounds like a quote from David H. Epp, born in 1861 and died in 1934," said Isaac.

"*Amigo*, did you memorize *all* the dates and quotes in Anabaptist History class last year?" Fabio asked Isaac.

"I'm sure he did," Alicia said. "He's a geek for facts and figures and quantum physics. And who knows what else he keeps in that brain of his!"

"All useful information for a future preacher." Isaac smiled. "I'll have to memorize the whole Bible, too, you know."

"No way!" Justin exclaimed. He twisted his mouth back and forth. "You're sure going to have a lot of lamps for your feet."

"Why would he have lamps for his feet?" Anna looked puzzled.

" 'Your word is a lamp to my feet and a light to my path,' Psalm 119:105," Li said, looking up from her digging. "It's a Bible verse. We learned it in Sunday school. Why don't you come to our class next Sunday? It's really cool. My mom can pick you up."

Isaac watched Alicia, who kept her head bowed as she chopped the earth with her hoe. Then she looked up. "Yeah, I think you would like it. It's not boring at all. We do lots of fun activities. And you could meet other kids in the neighborhood."

Anna looked at Alicia and Li, but didn't say anything.

"Campers, take a short break from digging and let me tell you about the hoes you're using. They have a story." Jesse held up his hoe for all to see.

"It was the year 1918, during World War I. Imagine a group of tents scattered around an army training camp in Chillicothe, Ohio." Jesse swung his free arm out in a half-circle. "One of your Mennonite faith ancestors was there."

"His name was Dan Stuckey," Christina joined in, "and he was one of more than a hundred conscientious objectors, called COs, at the camp. These men had been drafted into the army but refused to take combat training. 'You're a fine bunch of lousy rats,' the army lieutenant told them."

"When Dan was asked to carry a rifle and walk guard duty, he refused to carry a gun," Jesse told the campers. " 'Well, you wouldn't refuse to carry a hoe, now would you?' the lieutenant asked him. So Dan took his turn at guard duty, carrying a hoe."

"Do you think the other soldiers who carried guns laughed at Dan and insulted him?" Christina asked the campers.

"Sure," Anna blurted out. "I'm surprised they didn't torture him."

"Sometimes being peacemakers or standing up for their beliefs *did* cost our heroes their lives," Jesse said. "Thousands of our faith ancestors were burned, drowned, or hanged during the 16th century. Even today, Mennonites in Colombia, Iraq, and other countries have been murdered."

"Carrying a hoe instead of a rifle was humiliating, but it was a creative way to be a faithful peacemaker," Christina added. "Men like Dan planted a seed and made it possible for people in later wars to serve as conscientious objectors."

"I want to be a conscientious objector, a spy, a football player, and a teacher of peace," Justin declared. "And a cook."

"Bro, if you keep adding things to your list, you'll have to live to be 200 to get it all done!" teased Fabio.

"Since you want to be a doctor, you can help me live a really long life," Justin replied.

"I think my hoe just hit something," Li interrupted. "Hey, I found something!" she shouted.

"Okay, campers, let's see if Li found one of the treasures," said Jesse, running from the opposite side of the garden. Everyone gathered around Li as she stooped to pick up a green metal box from the rich black earth.

"Everyone ready for Li to open the box?"

"Yeah!" they shouted.

Li's eyes sparkled. The campers moved in closer as she removed the cover from the small box. She drew out a long tan thread and held it up.

"You look disappointed, Li," said Jesse.

"Yeah, big deal! A piece of thread." Anna voiced her opinion loud and clear. "I hope the other treasures aren't just a bunch of threads. Next thing, you'll be telling us we have to sew them all together."

Li looked again into the box's small opening and took out a tiny piece of crimson cloth, embroidered with a cross. Wrapped inside the cloth was a piece of glass and a message.

"Clue to campers," Li read. "Decode the meaning of the thread. Find the match to the cloth. Whoever solves the puzzle gets to dance with Isaac Thomas Roth."

The campers hooted with laughter. "Isaac Thomas doesn't know how to dance! Who would want to dance with *him*?"

Isaac's face turned the color of the crimson cloth.

"Just a minute, campers." Jesse raised his hand. "I want you to know that Christina and I asked Isaac first, before we put him on the spot like this. He didn't know all that we were planning, but he agreed to it anyway. Don't you think that took lots of courage?"

Justin looked over at Isaac. "Bro, that took guts."

"Man, that was a brave move. But I hope you'll let me teach you how to groove before you do the salsa." Fabio smiled at Isaac. "Give me five, bro!"

"Justin's right, campers. It took guts for Isaac to agree to be a dance partner. I'm sure he knew people would laugh at him, even his friends," Christina said.

"At camp this week, you're learning that peace takes guts," she continued. "Peacemakers choose to follow God's way. Often they're ridiculed, spit on, or beaten. Some are even killed. Peacemakers don't take the easy road. They take the Jesus road. And that makes all the difference in the way they live and die."

"Our faith heroes planted seeds of peacemaking for us," Jesse added. "Let's remember that as we plant our own seeds at Camp Amani Ya Juu."

"Seeds for the camp's peace feasts," Justin said. "I'm thinking of strawberries, watermelon, and broccoli with cheese."

Christina smiled at him. "Not just for the peace feasts, but for other surprises, too."

"Hey, Chris." Jesse winked at her. "Don't give away too many of our little camp secrets yet."

"Keep digging, campers." Christina smiled at Jesse. "The plot will get clearer. No pun intended. Li, you can put your mystery box in the ice chest over there. And would you please bring us some of the seed packets from the chest?"

"It's the peacemaker treasure chest," Justin said.

"I hit something!" one of the campers called out.

"Treasures are popping up everywhere!" Jesse exclaimed, running to the new find. "Gather 'round, campers."

The treasure finder leaned down and scooped up a clod of soil. He brushed off the dirt from a small wooden box and held it up for all to see. On the lid was a drawing, outlined in black and white finger paints.

"Anyone want to guess what the drawing is?" Christina asked.

"It looks like a table," said one of the campers.

"You're right. It *is* a table, a special table," said Christina. "And it represents a special story. Ready to open the box?"

"Yeah!" everyone shouted.

The camper first took out a long black thread and held it up, then a wad of paper and two pieces of wood, one dark and the other much lighter. He read the words written on the paper. "Clue to campers: Decode the meaning of the thread. Find the match to the wood. Whoever solves the puzzle gets to read a special book."

"Good job, campers. Keep digging. And let's start sowing these seeds." Christina held up packages of all sorts of seeds.

The campers soon found two more treasures in the garden's earth. These treasures, too, held colored threads, along with a rock and a feather. Soon all the seeds were planted, and the campers inserted a peace pole at the east end of the garden.

Then, hot, tired, and dirty, they followed Christina and Jesse to the trail that would lead them to lunch and an afternoon of swimming, canoeing, video lab, Bible study, photography, arts and crafts. Two campers carried the ice chest. Someone started chanting, "Yo, ho, ho, and a chest full of treasures." Another began to sing, "Oh when the saints go marching in." Alicia could hear Isaac's strong voice ahead, leading out with "Our God is an awesome God."

In all the excitement, no one missed Anna Bee.

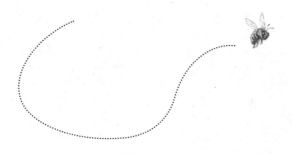

18

Mystery in the Forest

Anna hid in the tall pines around the garden and watched as the others disappeared on the trail heading back to camp, laughing and singing. She wasn't used to being around so many people at one time. Her house was quiet, and her dad spoke softly, with few words. Since her mom had been away, her brother didn't say much either. Anna smiled as she thought of her dad's nickname for her.

"You are our loud one," he would say. "You're sweet as a happy honey bee and loud as an angry bumble bee. You're our 'Little Buzzing Bee.'"

But Anna didn't feel like a buzzing bee today. She liked the quiet under the sturdy pines. The tops of the trees swayed gently in the wind. She could hear them whispering, high above her head. Anna walked farther into the cool forest. Soon she would join the others, but for now this would be her peaceful, private place to think about her mom. She wondered what she'd say when she saw her at the military prison.

Just east of her pine-needle path, Anna noticed a cluttered jumble of vines, bushes, and scrawny trees.

She stepped off the path and walked all around the tangled brush, but could see no way into it. She pulled apart a cluster of dead-looking vines with both hands and tried to get her foot into an opening. She thought for a moment, then lowered her shoulders and covered her eyes and head.

"Buzzing Bee, coming through!" she said. She pushed her body through the rough brush and found herself in the middle of vines and thorns and stinging nettles. The clump of dead, woody vines and slender green vines was stronger than it looked. "Aa-aa-ah!" she cried, trying to force her way through again. Her fingers were bloody, and her face felt like a mixture of sunburn and cat scratches. She was trapped!

"Pretend you're swimming on top of the deepest ocean," she remembered her mom saying. "If you get scared and thrash about, you'll sink. But if you relax and let God hold you, you'll float and be safe."

Anna smiled and relaxed. She took a deep breath, closed her eyes, and bowed her head. She could imagine herself floating on top of a gentle wave, high above the ocean floor. She felt lighter and freer.

Then she opened her eyes and saw below her in the brush a brown leather pouch, wedged between two large, dead vines. She bent over and reached for it. "Ouch! Stupid thorns," she cried.

Anna found a small stick and poked at the pouch. "Gotcha!" She grabbed it and brought it close to her face. Her back ached from being stuck in a bent-over position in the vines. She struggled to stand up.

The pouch felt smooth and worn. When Anna

opened it, she found old-looking stamps labeled "Sugar" and "Coffee." Behind them, she found a yellowed, creased note with faded handwriting, an ancient-looking map, and a tarnished silver key.

19

Day Three

On day three at Camp Amani Ya Juu, the campers gathered at the same spot on the park lawn. Again they sat on brightly colored quilts, and the counselors shouted out, "Welcome to Camp Amani Ya Juu!"

It was a lot like the other days, but something was different. Like the way Anna acted, and Alicia, too. They were actually talking and laughing together.

Isaac seemed quieter, but Li was joking more. Fabio was taking more time to listen. And Justin was handing out breakfast bars to everyone nearby.

"I said I was going to eat two breakfast bars this morning." Justin turned to Li and offered her one. "So I thought I might as well share a good thing with the other campers, too. They probably didn't eat enough breakfast, either. Breakfast is the most important meal, you know."

"I know. I have a bowl of rice every morning. And before you ask, no, I don't put cheese on it," Li teased.

"Mm-mm, melted cheddar cheese is so good on rice." Justin licked his lips.

"Bro, you need to come to *mi casa*. We put cheese on lots of things," put in Fabio. "And lots and lots of hot peppers."

"I don't like hot peppers much, but if they're covered with cheese, I guess they might be okay."

Fabio turned to Isaac. "Why so glum, chum?"

"I'm not glum. I'm just thinking about yesterday in the garden—seeds and roots and hidden treasures. It's so easy to miss God's treasures if we're not paying attention. Know what I mean?"

"Uh, no, not really. That's a little too much this early in the morning. But maybe we can talk later."

"Speaking of hidden treasures, fellow Menno Slick Sixers," Alicia said, "while we were singing and dancing along the trail back to camp yesterday, Anna found some more treasures."

Anna's eyes flashed. "I wanted to tell them myself."

"Oh, I'm sorry, Anna. I was so excited, I wanted to share it with everybody."

"Okay, but try not to let it happen again, if you want to be friends."

"What'd you find, Anna?" Justin asked excitedly.

"Let's meet over by the bridge on the way to the first activity, and I'll show you."

"Deal," said Fabio, stretching his hand, palm down, into the middle of their huddle. "Deal," agreed the others, placing their hands one by one on top of Fabio's.

"Okay, campers, we have a special treat for you today," announced Andi, one of the counselors.

"We're boarding a bus that will take us to the Mennonite History Museum. All of you have either planted a peace garden or cooked up a peace feast. Today's the day to solve the clues you found during those activities."

"An old, boring museum is a special treat?" Anna frowned and looked at Li.

"Any questions?" yelled Jesse.

"How are we going to solve the clues?" asked a camper.

"You'll find out at the museum."

"Who has the clues? Is somebody taking the clues?" someone else questioned.

"Look for Christina and Tim at the museum. They'll have all the clues."

"How soon are we leaving?" asked Anna. "Do we have time for a potty break?"

Several campers snickered.

Anna gave them a dirty look. "You don't even know why I asked that question, bird brains." She wanted to show the mystery map and old leather pouch to her new friends before they left on the bus. But now there wasn't enough time.

Last night she'd stared at the old map again and again and tried to decipher the strange, handwritten message on the yellowed slip of paper. She was hoping Isaac and the others could help her figure it out.

"Sorry, the bus is waiting," Andi called out. "There's a rest room on the bus. Or you can wait till we get to the museum."

Some of the campers snickered again.

Anna wrinkled up her nose and frowned. "Reptile brains," she muttered.

Just climbing on the bus, Anna quickly told her friends, "Let's meet on the bridge when we get back, and I'll show you what I found."

When they arrived at the museum, Christina and Tim were waiting at the entrance.

"Peace gardeners, please follow me," motioned Christina. "I have your treasure clues. We'll head to the left, inside these doors."

"Feast makers, I'm the master of hot leads today." Tim smiled and held up a bread basket. "Your clues are in here. Follow me, and you'll find what you seek."

The campers filed through the museum's tiled entrance. "Hey, look at the floor!" Li said. "It looks like the stepping stones on the bridge."

"Those images in the tiles are of our Anabaptist faith heroes," added Isaac.

"Hold the door, bro," Fabio told Justin. "Somebody just dropped something." Fabio leaned over to pick up a yellowed piece of paper with faded handwriting.

Christina stopped next to a cloth-paneled wall and turned around. "Okay, people of the peace garden. This is where we start our journey through the Mennonite History Museum." She held up four pieces of thread. "Here are the clues you dug up in the garden. Remember the colored threads—black, tan, red, and multi-colored?"

"Yeah, like I said yesterday, big deal, a bunch of thread," Anna muttered to herself.

"Threads of many colors make a coat of many colors," Isaac said, winking at Justin.

"Yeah, like Joseph's coat of many colors that his daddy gave him," Justin said. "His brothers got real jealous."

Jesse walked up and cleared his throat. "And campers, don't forget the other clues. Like the little painted box that held the black thread." He held up the box. "And we have pieces of dark and light wood, a piece of glass, a rock, a feather, and a crimson cloth with a cross."

"All of these clues point to heroes and stories that can be found inside this museum," Christina added. "Take a good look at the clues before you start looking for their matches."

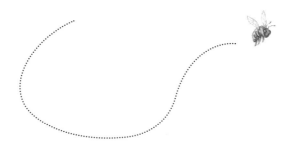

20

Treasures at the Museum

The campers moved from wall to wall of the museum, through the neatly arranged displays. They read signs and peered into glass-covered cases. They touched quilts, baby dolls, and clocks with weird faces. They passed by tables and beds and old, old photographs.

Li saw it first—a large dining table, half of it made from dark wood and half of it from light wood. She remembered the pieces of wood in the little box with the picture of a table on the lid.

"I found it! I found a match," she called out.

Christina, Jesse, and the other campers crowded around Li and the table.

"Which puzzle does this solve?" Jesse asked her.

"The little box with the table painted on its lid. It had pieces of dark and light wood, like this table here."

"Does anyone know the story about this table?" Christina asked.

"I think I do," answered Alicia. "There was a table like this one in Atlanta, Georgia, during the Civil Rights movement. It was at the Mennonite House in downtown Atlanta. Black and white people and probably other colors of people all ate around the table. Coretta Scott King ate at the table. They worshipped around it, too. Lots of Mennonite volunteers worked in Atlanta during that time."

"I was at the junior youth convention in Atlanta," Isaac spoke up, "and they had a replica of the table there. It was a sign of unity during the Civil Rights movement, and it's a sign of unity for Mennonites now. All people are welcome at God's table."

"Let's look at the museum's description," suggested Christina. Turning to a bronze plaque on the wall, she asked, "Fabio, would you read this to us?"

"Sure," he answered, then read slowly and clearly. "Rosemarie Freeney Harding and Vincent Harding established the first interracial community center in Atlanta, Georgia, in 1961, working with Mennonite Central Committee.

"Here's a quote," he went on. "'You are the ones who are going to sustain this country and this world. There is no other way than peace. If there is any time that the Anabaptist movement needs to work, it is now. We must keep the sharpness of the Anabaptist core of peace and reconciliation.' It's signed 'Rosemarie Harding, 2003.' "

"Wise words to remember, campers," said Christina. "We'll talk more about this tomorrow during round-up time."

"Li, congratulations! You solved the first puzzle. Remember the prize?" asked Jesse. "'Whoever finds the match to the wood gets to read a special book.' The museum has a copy of *Martyrs Mirror* for you to take home, Li."

"*Marty's Mirror*?" asked Anna. "Is that a teen novel?" She looked at Alicia. "I didn't know stuffy old museums had teen novels to check out! Can I get one? I need something to read tomorrow."

"I'll let you borrow my copy." Li giggled.

Alicia giggled, too. "But it's pretty long. We'd better get you something else to read tomorrow. Where will you be, anyway? You're coming to camp, aren't you?"

"I can't come to camp tomorrow. I'm going to visit my mom."

"In prison?" asked Alicia.

"Yeah, and you don't have to tell the whole world, either," Anna snapped. "It's none of their beeswax!"

"Sorry, Anna. I wasn't trying to broadcast it. You know, you might need to work on your anger a little."

"Yeah, like you don't have any anger at all, Miss Priss. Justin told me all about how angry you are at God because your mom died."

Alicia's dark eyes bored into Anna. She was about to reply, but Christina was herding the group somewhere else. "Let's continue with our tour," she said. "Oh, we forgot something, campers." She held up one of the threads she had shown to them earlier.

"Ready to guess what the black thread means?"

No one said anything.

Then Justin spoke. "That the coat of many colors has some black thread in it?"

Everyone laughed.

"Well, yes, you could say that," said Christina. "Want to say more?"

"Uh, no, that's all."

"Well, everyone, be thinking about the threads we found. The meaning will become clearer as you solve the other puzzles. Let's keep moving. Who'll be the next puzzle solver?"

The campers found a room with a rowboat hanging from the ceiling. "Man, that's cool." Fabio stood for several moments looking up at the boat's underside. He didn't notice that the others had gone on without him. He walked fast and caught up with the group as they entered a huge hall of photographs and paintings—hundreds of them. Some were black and white, others in full color. A huge banner identified this section as "Our Family."

Li walked toward the east wall. "This is most beautiful," she said softly, staring at a painting. She motioned to Alicia to come over.

"This painting is done in traditional Chinese style," she told her friend. "The inscription says it's by Lien-Nu Huang from Taichung, Taiwan. I wonder if she is Mennonite, too, like me."

"Yes, she is," answered a man's voice behind her.

"Campers, this is Mr. Ben Dirks, director of the museum," introduced Christina. "Mr. Dirks has traveled all over the world collecting information, photos, and videos for this exhibit. Some people learn about his work and send the museum special items like this painting."

Mr. Dirks smiled. "When I go to a country, I stay with a Mennonite family. I get to know them, go to work with them, hang out with the kids, eat foods I'm not used to, visit interesting places, and go to church. I take lots of photographs and video tape, too," he added. "Once I videotaped from the back of a motorcycle in some wild traffic in India!"

"Cool!" said Justin. "I like motorcycles."

Mr. Dirks went on. "I wanted this exhibit to show that all people are created in God's image, that we're all equal. And that in our Mennonite and Anabaptist family, we can celebrate our differences and similarities."

"I want to be a museum director, conscientious objector, football player, spy, and peace teacher," Justin whispered to Fabio.

"And a cook, too, remember?"

"Oh yeah, a cook, too," Justin agreed, nodding vigorously.

"When you get to the end of this hall," Mr. Dirks said, "take a right and you'll see a wall of videos from my travels. Check out the ceiling too."

Justin and Fabio reached the video wall first. "Wow, bro, look at that motorcycle go!" Fabio pointed to one of the moving images on the wall. "Mr. Dirks is on the back of that thing. Look how he's wobbling. It's a wonder he didn't drop his camera!"

"Mr. Dirks wasn't the only one with a camera," said Justin. "Somebody's videotaping him—look! Like me recording Anna with Jacques Dosie at the castle. We've gotta show you that video, Fabio."

"Yeah, man, I heard you talking about that castle thing. You and Anna didn't eat any of those wild berries on the vines that were covering the bridge, did you? Sometimes weird fruit can make you hallucinate and see strange things."

"No! We didn't eat any weird fruit. I showed the video to Alicia. *She* believes it's for real. You'll just have to see it, Fabio."

"Okay, okay, bro. I'll take your word for it. Maybe we can all meet at my house Saturday night and watch the video then. Mom'll be back from the disabilities retreat. I'll ask her if you guys can come over for supper."

Justin smiled. "Has your mom been gone all week? Do you miss her? I miss my mom."

"Yeah, she and Celia left last Sunday. They go to the retreat every year. Celia loves it. I miss both of them. We're having a piñata birthday party for Celia when they get home. She'll be 23, but she still loves piñatas like a little kid."

"I like Celia," Justin said. "She gives me a big hug every time I see her."

He looked up at the video on the ceiling. "Hey, look up there. What are those kids building?"

"Looks like some kind of shed," answered Fabio. "And some of them are landscaping a yard."

"Yeah, they must be using that big pile of rocks. Look, they're jumping on the pile and sliding down it. Ha!" Justin twisted his mouth, thinking. Something

109

was niggling at his brain. Suddenly, it hit him. "*Rocks!* That's one of the clues. Hey, I found a clue, everybody! Look at the rocks on the ceiling."

Jesse, Christina, and the other campers looked up, where Justin was pointing.

"Let's push this button and see what the video's all about," Jesse suggested.

A woman's crisp voice came over the speaker system. "In the summer of 2004, six youth groups from Canada's Region Five built 25 garden sheds for the survivors of a firestorm in Louis Creek and Barriere, British Columbia. They also landscaped yards and listened to survivors tell their stories."

One guy on the video slid down the rock pile and shoved his face in the camera. "We're tired but happy," he shouted at the lens. "We've built 300 garden sheds!"

"No, we didn't, dude, we built 25," another youth disagreed.

"That's right," added a girl. "And we've been landscaping yards, too. This is more fun than going to Disney World. And so much more meaningful. I think we're doing what Jesus would do."

"I think Jesus would go to Disney World, too," Anna spoke up. "He liked to have a good time, didn't he? He could work on sheds in the daytime and ride on roller coasters at night."

"Do you like roller coasters?" Alicia asked.

"I LOVE roller coasters."

"Me too," Alicia said. "Maybe you can come with Justin and me, next time Dad takes us."

"Thanks. I'll think about it," Anna said, sticking her hand in a pocket of her shorts. Something was missing!

Jesse's voice interrupted her thoughts. "Campers, Justin's solved the puzzle of the rocks. Remember the clue? 'Find the match to the rock. Whoever solves it gets to eat their favorite food from a crock.'"

"We know what *that's* going to be!" shouted several of the campers. "Cheese!" Everyone laughed.

Anna started pulling her pockets inside out. She checked her front, then her back pockets. She couldn't find it! The handwritten message she'd found in the leather pouch from the forest was gone.

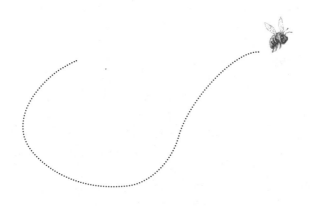

21

The Door in the Floor

Anna spun around, and sped back through the hall of photographs and paintings. Looking down, she swept the floor with her eyes from right to left, left to right. She ran through the room with the boat. She dashed past the baby dolls and clocks and glass-covered cases, through displays of turn-of-the-century quilts, linens, and silk. Out of breath, she stopped in front of the two-toned table. Nothing! She'd found nothing.

"It was a code. I *know* it was a code," she said. "Why do I have to be such a bird-brain and lose it?" She opened the leather pouch and took out the creased map. She unfolded it and spread it on the table. It looked like lots of little rooms in a big building. But *what* building? A bank? A school? She didn't know any big building with lots of little rooms.

Anna folded the map and held it in her hand. She started toward the front door, retracing more of her steps. Just before she got to the entrance, she noticed an opening on her left, with a sign, "Display temporarily closed for renovations."

"Well, I *know* I didn't go in there," she said to her-self. "I lost the paper. I lost the code. That's all there is to it." She turned to go back and find the others, and saw Alicia, Fabio, Li, Isaac, and Justin hurrying toward her.

"Where have you been? We thought you disap-peared into thin air," Alicia scolded.

"No need to be a drama queen," Anna retorted. "I lost the piece of paper I found yesterday and was try-ing to find it, that's all."

"We were worried about you. We thought you got mad about something and took off," Li said.

"You're one of us now. We care about you," Isaac added. "The Menno Slick Six, remember?"

Justin was deep in thought. "Fabio, didn't you pick up a piece of paper by the front door? Maybe it was Anna's."

"Oh yeah, I did pick up a piece of paper! I think I still have it." Fabio reached into his pocket. "Here it is."

"That's it!" cried Anna. She took the paper and danced a step. "There *is* a God! Thank you, Jesus!"

The others looked at each other and smiled. "Our spiritual side must've rubbed off on you, girl. You're saying God and Jesus, all in one breath," Alicia teased.

"We'd better get back to the others," Isaac said. "We'll meet on the bridge later and look at Anna's paper."

Bam! Bam! Bam!

"What's that?" Fabio looked around as they turned toward the sound coming from their left.

Bam! Bam! Bam! "Can anyone hear me?"

"Was that a voice?"

Bam! Bam! Bam! "Anyone there? Help me, please!"

"It *is* a voice, and it's coming from in there." Justin pointed to the room under renovation.

"Come on, everybody! Duck under the rope," Anna said, scooting under herself.

Bam! Bam! Bam! Bam! "Please help me!"

"We hear you! Where are you?" Isaac yelled.

"Under the stairway. There's a door in the floor."

"Look—over there!" Li pointed toward the stairs in a corner of the room.

Bam! Bam! Bam! "Over here!"

"We're coming!" yelled Fabio.

"Look, there's the door in the floor. Pull up on that hook," Alicia instructed Isaac.

"Got it." Isaac strained to pull the small hook up and out. "Rats!" The hook broke in his hands. "Now what'll we do? There's no other handle."

"Did the hook break off? Oh no," said the voice beneath the door.

"Okay, let's keep cool," said Li. "Look around for something else to pry open the door."

"We might have to get help," Anna said.

"Wait a minute. What about this thing over here?" Justin saw a long silver pipe with a hook on the end.

"I think that'll work," said Isaac. "They use it to get quilts down that are too high to reach. Let's try it."

"Are you there? Can you get help?" pleaded the voice below the floor.

Isaac poked the hook of the long pipe into the tiny opening in the door. "Rats and bats! I can't get it to catch," he said.

"Here, let me try," Li offered. She moved the pipe into place and gently pushed the hook into the opening, then slowly pulled up on the door. The hook came loose.

"Oh, man. This isn't going to work," Fabio said, shaking his head.

"If at first you don't succeed, try again." Li said. She hooked the door again, pulled on it slowly, and a large gloved hand appeared in the opening.

"Aa-ah!" they all screamed.

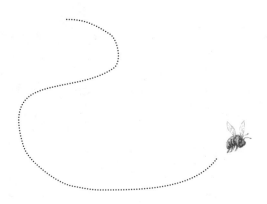

22

Into the Basement

I t's just me, Ben Dirks," said the voice, as two hands grabbed hold of the sides of the opening. Soon Mr. Dirks' head emerged.

"What happened?" Alicia asked.

"I didn't use the sense God gave me," he replied. "I didn't tell anyone where I was going. And that heavy trap door fell back into the opening before I could get it secured on the other side. Thank goodness you students heard me, or I may have been spending a night at the museum."

"There *is* a God! Thank you, Jesus," Justin said, grinning at Anna.

"What's down there, anyway?" Anna tried to peek down the dark hole.

"A long flight of stairs," said Mr. Dirks. "They lead to our climate-controlled basement storage area for rare artifacts and other items we're holding for display. It keeps them safe from dust and breakage while we make a place for them up top."

"Could we go down there to look? Please?" Anna asked.

"I don't know about that, young lady," answered Mr. Dirks. "You should probably get back to the others. They'll be wondering where you are."

"It's a great chance to share more about Anabaptist history with us, Mr. Dirks," coaxed Isaac. "And since Anna is new to all this, I'm sure she'd learn a lot."

"Um-mm, well, maybe you're right, Isaac. You obviously have some of your mother's 'persuasive lawyer' skills. You campers will be the first to experience a basement tour here." He smiled and gestured toward the steps. "But I should let someone know before we all go down. There's a phone over on the wall. I'll go and give Christina a call."

"Can you believe we found this secret passageway?" Anna said, looking at the others.

"Well, it's not really secret," Alicia said, "but we can pretend."

"Yeah! I like secrets and dark holes and long, winding stairways," Justin said.

Mr. Dirks returned from his phone call. "Okay, campers, we're ready to go down," he said. "Please be careful on the steps! Hold onto the railing. The steps are wide, but the light's dim. That's another thing I need to take care of—better lighting on this stairway."

"This is so cool," said Justin, as they made their way down the long stairway to the basement.

"Better than Disney World," said Anna.

"Everyone wait for me at the bottom of the stairs," instructed Mr. Dirks.

"It's dark down here," said Alicia. "I don't like dark places."

"Hold on, campers. There's a light I can turn on when I get to the bottom," said Mr. Dirks. He stepped onto the cool, concrete floor and reached for a switch. "There, that's better."

"Man, there's a lot of stuff down here," Fabio said.

"Where did it come from?" asked Li.

"From all over the world," said Mr. Dirks. "Each item has a story to tell about our Mennonite heritage. Just look over here at these quilts and tapestries." He motioned for them to follow him. "Some are from Russia, some from Germany. Others are from the Netherlands and Switzerland. Some of the quilts are newer and are replicas of ones we already have on display."

"What's this one?" asked Fabio.

"That's a newer quilt. We have another one just like it on display in the hall of quilts upstairs. Did you walk through that part of the museum?"

"No, we didn't get to that part yet," answered Isaac.

"Well then, I can tell you about some of the quilts. This one that you asked about tells the story of Javier Segura Gonzales. He was a Mennonite pastor in Bogotá, Colombia—the first Mennonite pastor to lose his life due to violence in his country."

Fabio examined the face on the quilt.

"Javier was only 31 when he was killed by a bomb that exploded near him," Mr. Dirks went on.

"There's too much violence in Colombia," Fabio said. "Who would want to lead a church there, when there's so much hatred in that country?"

"That's a good question," responded Mr. Dirks. "A woman who attended Javier's funeral told us that his fiancée spoke and assured the hundreds of mourners that God would carry the church forward. The report we heard said the mourners prayed to God for peace in their city and for forgiveness for those who killed Javier. Javier's death wasn't the final chapter of the peace witness in Colombia."

Mr. Dirks pointed to the quilt. "Notice the cross and the torch embroidered in the quilt. Followers of Jesus carry the torch of faith. God makes it possible to hope for a peaceful and just society in Colombia. By sharing Javier's story, we can be part of carrying the torch for peace and justice."

"Why does the quilt show pieces of broken glass everywhere?" Fabio asked. "And what does the rose mean?"

"More good questions," Mr. Dirks said. "The broken glass represents violence and death. The rose is a symbol of life and love, of hope and beauty."

"It's almost like the broken glass and the rose are fighting each other to see who will win," said Anna.

"Hey! What were those clues in the green metal box we found in the garden?" Fabio looked like a light had just turned on in his head.

"There was a tan thread and a piece of crimson cloth with a cross on it," Li said. "A small bit of glass was in there, too. Wow! I think you just solved one of the puzzles, Fabio."

"Is that the one where the solver gets to dance with Isaac Thomas Roth?" Fabio laughed.

"Yes, it is, bro. You were going to teach me to salsa, remember?" Isaac grinned.

"Maybe someone else will figure it out, too, since there's an identical quilt on display upstairs," Alicia pointed out. "Then you'll have two dancing partners, Isaac."

"Did anybody figure out what the colored threads mean?" Justin reminded them.

"Nope, forgot all about it," said Isaac. "How about you, Justin? Are you sticking with your 'coat of many colors' theory?"

"For now, but I'm still thinking about it."

Anna had left the others as they joked about Isaac's dancing partners. She walked in the dim light toward the other end of the hanging quilts.

"Mr. Dirks, who's this?" she called from the other end.

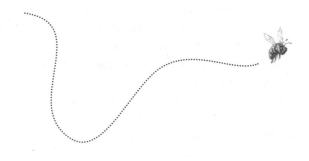

23

War and Peace

The others walked toward Anna, and she stepped back from the face on the quilt, so they could see it.

"Isn't that a beautiful quilt?" asked Mr. Dirks.

"Yeah, it's cool," Anna said.

"That's the Cheyenne peace chief, Lawrence Hart," Mr. Dirks said, smiling at Anna. "Since you know my name, may I ask yours?"

"Anna Bee."

"Anna Bee," he repeated. "I like that name. Are you enjoying camp this week, Anna?"

"Yeah, it's all right."

"Do you go to the same church as Isaac?"

"I don't go to any church. My dad and brother and me just moved here."

"Well, I'm glad you're at camp this week, Anna. And I'm especially glad you're visiting the museum. It's nice to meet you. Do you want to hear the story of Lawrence Hart? And why he's on this special quilt in a Mennonite museum?"

"Yeah, sure, I guess so. I want to know about that

other stuff on the quilt, too," Anna said, pointing to an airplane and a black beaver. "Oh, and the head-dress."

Mr. Dirks smiled and nodded. The other kids gathered around Anna. They were all looking at the snow-white quilt with its image of a calm-eyed man. His broad shoulders were draped in a colorful Native American blanket. Smaller images of an airplane, a black beaver, and a feather headdress surrounded him.

"Why don't we sit down here, in front of the quilt?" Mr. Dirks pointed to the floor. "Wait, and I'll get a blanket to sit on. Then I'll tell you how this amazing man became a chief of peace in the Mennonite church."

"Isaac, I bet you already know this story, don't you?" Justin asked, looking at the face on the quilt and then at Isaac.

"I think I know part of the story, but probably not all of it," Isaac replied. "I met Chief Lawrence Hart at a Mennonite peace gathering in Oklahoma. Native Americans have been part of Mennonite history longer than most people think."

Mr. Dirks spread a super-sized blanket on the concrete floor, and they all sat down.

"Okay, campers, let's start with Chief Lawrence Hart's story when he was a young boy. Everyone comfortable?"

"Snug as a bug in a rug," answered Justin, who had wrapped one piece of the huge blanket around his shoulders.

"Once there was a Cheyenne boy called Black

Beaver," began Mr. Dirks. "His grandfather gave him that name."

Anna smiled at the black beaver on the quilt.

"Black Beaver grew up in his grandfather's home, and he loved him. The old man was a Cheyenne chief and told Black Beaver many stories about his brave people. The tribe's warriors fought with great courage. But the bravest of all, said his grandfather, were the chiefs who believed in peace. Black Beaver loved to hear his grandfather talk about the peace chiefs, but he was sorry that there were no warriors anymore. He wished he could become one.

"One hot day, Black Beaver was picking cotton. He lay down on his cotton sack to rest for a while and look up into the blue sky. Suddenly he heard a roaring noise. A group of airplanes swept above him in perfect formation and disappeared into the distance.

"In that instant, Black Beaver knew what he wanted to do. He would take his English name and become Lawrence Hart, the great pilot. He would fight like the brave Cheyenne warriors in the past."

Anna pointed to the airplane embroidered on the quilt. "Did he become a bomber pilot? That looks like a military plane."

"The story will tell you," Mr. Dirks said with a smile. Then he went on.

"Lawrence needed to go to college to prepare to become a pilot, and the pastor of his church in Oklahoma encouraged him to go to Bethel College in Kansas. Lawrence soon found that this college emphasized serving others and making peace. But he didn't pay much attention. After all, he was planning to go into the military and become a great pilot."

Anna interrupted. "I'd like to become a pilot some day—fly high above the clouds and be totally surrounded by blue sky."

Mr. Dirks shifted his position on the floor and continued. "At Bethel College, Lawrence met a student named Larry Kaufman. They became close friends. Larry told Lawrence his dream of going into mission work. He was against war and violence. Lawrence shared his dream of becoming a great pilot in the air force. He wanted the members of his tribe to be proud of him."

"Their dreams were opposites," put in Li.

"That's right, but it didn't matter. Larry and Lawrence were friends. They listened to each other and respected each other's views.

"After two years, the friends went in opposite directions. Larry went to Africa to work with the Congo Inland Mission. Lawrence went on to study to be a pilot. He worked hard and studied math and physics."

"*Quantum* physics?" questioned Alicia.

"I'm not sure about that," replied Mr. Dirks, "but he studied everything he needed to become a great pilot, including the technical systems that go into aircraft. Finally, he reached his goal. He became a pilot, then a marine pilot, then a jet fighter pilot, and finally a special weapons pilot.

"Lawrence was tutored by the best fliers of the Korean War. They showed a film to teach him how to

124

deliver special weapons of destruction. The film showed planes and pilots being shot down. The scenes were horrible. Lawrence was shocked when he saw what it was like to kill people. He knew that as a pilot in the war he could be shooting women and children and other innocent people, just like his own Cheyenne people had been brutally shot down by soldiers. It made him think, was this really what he wanted to do? In the midst of his struggle he heard sad news. His friend, Larry Kaufman, had died while doing his peaceful mission work in Africa.

"Memories of Larry rushed into his mind—what his friend believed, and the good things he hoped to do. He remembered hearing about the great Cheyenne peace chiefs from his grandfather."

"What did he do?" asked Alicia, learning forward. "Did he join the Congo Inland Mission like his friend?"

"No, but Lawrence did receive a new vision, one that was just for him. He left the air force as soon as possible. He studied to be a minister, and became pastor of his home church in Oklahoma. His tribe respected him highly and made him a Cheyenne chief. During a special ceremony, his mother gave him a new name, Chief-in-the-Sky."

"Man, that's a cool name. I like that," said Fabio.

"Mr. Dirks, did you know that the peace chief tradition goes back hundreds of years to a Cheyenne chief named Sweet Medicine?" Isaac asked. "He taught that a peace chief must be a peacemaker, no matter what the cost. Peace chiefs never took up arms, even in self-defense."

"Yes, I've read about Chief Sweet Medicine," answered Mr. Dirks. "Thank you for sharing that information, Isaac. That sounds like our Anabaptist ancestors, doesn't it? Martyrs like Felix Manz, Michael Sattler, Maeykyn Wens, and so many others refused to take up arms to defend themselves, and they died for their beliefs."

"We met Adriaen and Hans Wens right after their mother had been burned at the stake," Justin blurted out. "When Adriaen said goodbye to us and took his little brother Hans home, it made us all cry."

The other kids froze like statues and looked at Mr. Dirks, wondering what he'd say. Isaac leaned over and whispered in Justin's ear. "Adults will think we're crazy if we tell them about our time travel episodes. Try to keep your lips zipped."

"I didn't know you were performing plays at camp," said Mr. Dirks. "That's an excellent idea. Sounds like it really made history come alive for you. Maybe we should have some of those performances at the museum sometime."

"Uh, yeah," Isaac replied. Then he changed the subject. "Mr. Dirks, you said there were some items down here from Switzerland and the Netherlands and other European countries. Could you show us those?"

"Of course! I'm so glad you're interested in Mennonite history. Follow me, and I'll show you some beautiful tapestries that were recently donated to the museum."

The Menno Slick Six followed Mr. Dirks through rows of quilts, wall hangings, and other items, large and small.

Suddenly, Anna, who was just behind Mr. Dirks, turned around and stopped the others. "Wouldn't it be cool to live down here for a while?" she asked, her eyes glowing in the dim light. "I'll bet there are some secret passageways around here."

"And long, narrow, winding staircases," Justin said.

"And hidden panels in the walls," Fabio added.

"And bodyless heads that roam the darkened passages, stairways, and hidden panels," Isaac spoke in a spooky voice, as he poked Alicia from behind.

"Aa-ah!" screamed Alicia.

"Stop it, all of you!" Li scolded. "Mr. Dirks is waiting for us."

"Hello, campers, over here," Mr. Dirks said.

Suddenly, everything went black.

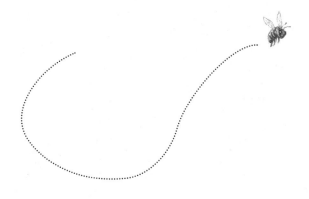

24

The Tapestries

Aa-aah!" several voices screamed at the same time. "Oh, sorry," said Mr. Dirks. "I must've hit the timer instead of the switch when we first came down. Hold on, I've got a flashlight."

A narrow beam of light shone on the floor. "Just follow the light to me."

"A light unto my path," Isaac said.

"And a lamp unto my feet," Justin added. "Psalm 119:105. Do we know the Bible or what, bro?"

"The real question is, do we know Jesus? And do we follow *his* path?" Isaac turned to Justin and smiled.

"I'll have to think about that," Justin said.

"I'm sorry about the blackout," Mr. Dirks said.

"I like blackouts," said Anna.

"I bet you'd like lock-ins, too," Fabio said.

"That's not funny, meathead!"

"Wait a minute, Anna. Do you know what a lock-in is? It's fun. Our youth group has one at the YMCA every year. We eat and swim and play games. What did you think?"

"A lock-in is a prison. *That's* what I think." Anna glared at Fabio in the flashlight's beam.

"Sorry, I didn't mean it that way at all. Chill out, will you?"

Mr. Dirks cleared his throat. "We'd better head back upstairs after I show you a few of these antique tapestries. I'm sorry you won't be able to see them very well. I hope you come back to the museum when they're on display upstairs. These are our most valuable museum pieces, and we're fortunate to have them."

Mr. Dirks shone his flashlight up and down four huge tapestries. Images of four bearded men shone back at them. Alicia gasped.

"Are you all right?" Mr. Dirks squinted into the dim light.

Alicia was shaking. She recognized the four tapestries. They were the same ones that were hanging from the carousel, the ones that had taken her and Isaac into another time. Her voice trembled as she asked, "That one's Felix Manz, isn't it? Where did you get these, Mr. Dirks? And who are the other people?"

"This collection was given by a donor from Europe. The person to the right of Felix Manz is Conrad Grebel, a co-worker of Manz during the birth of the Anabaptist movement. The next one, here, is George Blaurock, another of the early Anabaptist leaders. These three men," Mr. Dirks said, shining the flashlight beam over the faces, "lived in Switzerland."

"I know a lot about Felix Manz," Alicia told Mr. Dirks, "but could you tell us more about Conrad Grebel and George Blaurock?"

"Certainly," replied Mr. Dirks. "Follow me."

Alicia was first in line this time as Mr. Dirks led the way between tall stacks of old books, magazines, and newspapers. The others followed closely. Finally, they stopped before a massive antique door with a large scroll carved into its center panel. Mr. Dirks took a large silver key from his pocket and put it in the keyhole.

As he opened the door slowly, it creaked and groaned.

"That sounds spooky," said Anna, as the kids followed him into the small room.

"This is an excellent place for stories," said Mr. Dirks. "I'm assembling these sixteenth century bricks into a fireplace like the one used by Michael and Margaretha Sattler, two more Anabaptist heroes. There are just a few bricks missing. I'm traveling to Switzerland next year to meet with a man who may have the rest of them."

"Wow, these are really from the sixteenth century?" Alicia asked.

"Yes. And when we have all the bricks, we'll put them together as a complete fireplace upstairs. We're working on a new display area for storytelling and plays. It will make history come alive, just like your plays at camp."

Justin leaned over to Fabio and whispered, "If he only knew what was *really* making history come alive for us."

"Please have a seat." Mr. Dirks pointed to the floor in front of the partially assembled fireplace.

"You can pretend there's a warm fire. You're probably getting a bit chilly down here," he added. He took a blanket from the shelf behind him and spread it on the floor, then sat down nearest to the fireplace.

"Alicia asked for more information about Conrad Grebel and George Blaurock, two of the men on the tapestries. I'll tell you about them through a story," said Mr. Dirks. "Is everyone comfortable?"

"Yes!"

"The story begins like this . . . Conrad Grebel got in trouble as a young man, for fighting and living carelessly. But when he married, he became a Christian. He and his friends began a Bible study and discovered that the rules the churches followed were not in the Bible.

"For instance, church law said that infants must be baptized to save their souls. But Conrad and his friends couldn't find any story in the Bible about a baby being baptized.

"From studying the Bible, they believed that baptism marks our decision to follow Jesus. Only people who are old enough to think for themselves can make such a serious decision. But when Conrad and his Bible-study friends spoke out against the baptism of babies, several of them were put in jail."

"Those anti-Baptists spent a lot of time in jail, didn't they?" asked Anna.

"*Ana*baptists," corrected Alicia, "not *anti*-Baptists."

"Yeah, right, whatever they were," said Anna.

"I'm afraid they did spend a lot of time in jail," agreed Mr. Dirks, "but they are still showing us today that it takes guts to stand up for our beliefs and for the way of peace. They stood firm, even if it meant going to jail or being put to death.

"Conrad and his wife, Barbara, had a baby girl," he went on. "They went against the law and refused to baptize her. They didn't think a tiny baby could decide if she wanted to follow Jesus. The authorities told them if the baby wasn't baptized, they would have to leave their home and lose all they owned.

"Conrad and Barbara wondered what they should do. If they disobeyed the government, where would they live? How would they take care of their baby? Could they trust God to care for them? The Grebels turned to their good friend, George Blaurock. George was a tall, powerful man with sparkling eyes and black hair. According to the stories, people called him *Blaurock*, which means 'blue coat' in German, because he wore a blue coat."

"Was a piece of blue thread one of our clues?" Justin whispered to Isaac.

"No, dude—black, tan, red, and multicolored. No blues," answered Isaac.

"George Blaurock was born in Switzerland in 1491," Mr. Dirks continued. "When he grew up, he became a priest in the Catholic Church, but he began to disagree with the practice of baptizing babies. He left the Catholic Church, married, and moved to Zurich, Switzerland, where he met Conrad. They became good friends and studied the Bible together.

"On the day in 1525 that the government told Conrad and Barbara they must have their baby girl baptized, Conrad, George, and other friends walked quietly through the snow. They met secretly in a home to pray together and talk about what to do.

"At the beginning of the meeting, the men were sad. They knelt to pray, asking for God's will to be shown to them, and for the strength to follow it. They knew they would have to suffer if they disobeyed the government."

Bam! Bam! Bam!

"Aa-a-ah!" Everyone, including Mr. Dirks, screamed. The door to the room opened slowly, creaking and groaning. They all stared at it, frozen in their places.

"Oh, there you are, Mr. Dirks," said a tall boy with wire-rim glasses. "Sorry to disturb you, but we have a little problem upstairs. The boy's rest room is overflowing."

"Uh-oh," said Mr. Dirks. "I'll be right up. Would you campers like to wait here or head back up upstairs? I should only be a few minutes."

"We'll stay here," offered Anna.

"Right," added Isaac, Justin, and Fabio.

"That's okay with me, too," said Li.

"I'll go upstairs with you, Mr. Dirks," said Alicia.

"Oh, please stay, Alicia," said Anna. "We should all stick together."

"She's right. The Menno Slick Six should stay together," Justin said.

"Oh, okay . . . I guess you're right, Justin. I shouldn't leave you behind with this crew, anyway. No telling where you'd end up."

25

Hidden Passageway

"Man, can you believe these bricks are 500 years old? That's so cool," said Fabio, lightly touching some of the bricks in the fireplace.

"I wonder if anything else in here is that old," said Anna. "Maybe there's pirate gold hidden down here."

"Girl, what's wrong with you? This is a *peace* museum, not a pirate museum," Alicia said, rolling her eyes.

"If there were a secret hiding place in here, I wonder where it'd be," said Li.

"Beneath the floor," said Fabio. "That's where we found Mr. Dirks anyway." He laughed.

"Or maybe at the back of a closet, like in *The Chronicles of Narnia*," added Isaac.

"Except there are no closets in this little room," said Alicia.

"How about a hidden panel in the wall?" asked Anna, pressing on the wall behind her.

"No, that's too obvious," said Isaac. "You have to think like a spy. For instance, why is this cord over here? Could it be like the vine and take us to unknown worlds and even galaxies? And if scientists are correct about the black hole . . ."

"Where's Anna, everybody?" interrupted Justin.

Isaac, Alicia, Li, and Fabio turned toward the wall where Anna had just been.

"She disappeared again!" exclaimed Isaac.

"You don't think she went through that wall, do you?" asked Li.

"Maybe she was right about a hidden panel," said Justin.

"There's only one way to find out. Let's start pressing on the wall," said Alicia. "Everybody hold hands, to stay together. Here we go."

She pushed on the wall to the right of the fireplace, and it began to rotate, slowly and silently. When it stopped, they were in a narrow passageway, like a tunnel, with hanging quilts on each side.

"Whoa, it smells musty back here," said Fabio. "And it's downright cold!"

"Where's Anna?" asked Justin. "Does anyone see Anna?"

The five kids crept down the narrow hall, one after the other.

"Stick together now," said Alicia, turning around to make sure they all heard her.

"Do we have a choice?" retorted Isaac.

Alicia took another step and started sliding down a long chute.

"*AA-AA-AH!*" she screamed along with the others, who were sliding feet-first behind her.

"Sh-h-h!" said a strange man, who helped Alicia

to her feet at the bottom of the chute. "They are still in prayer. Please be quiet. From whence do you come?"

"Uh, we come from the upper room." Alicia pointed toward the ceiling.

"How many are with you?"

"Five, but we're looking for another person from our group."

"Did you see any government authorities on your way here?"

"No, just Mr. Dirks." Alicia's eyes had adjusted to the dim light, and she could see that they were in another time and place once again.

Justin, Fabio, Li, and Isaac followed Alicia and the man into a cozy room with a blazing fireplace. Several men in old-fashioned coats and knee pants and women in long dresses were seated with bowed heads. Two men were on their knees in the middle of the room. Alicia saw Anna seated in a row of chairs behind the strange-looking people. She led the others toward Anna, and they sat down.

"I know this scene," whispered Isaac to the others. "It's 1525, and we're in Switzerland."

"Sh-h-h!" whispered Anna. "Can't you see they're praying?"

After a long silence, the two men in the middle of the room stood up.

"That looks like the two men Mr. Dirks was telling us about," whispered Alicia.

"Yeah, one of them has a blue coat—that's George Blaurock," said Justin.

"The other one must be Conrad Grebel," said Li.

"Sh-h-h! They're talking," Anna hissed. "Listen."

"My faith is in Jesus Christ only," said George Blaurock to Conrad Grebel. "I ask that you baptize me now." George knelt before his friend, and Conrad poured water from a dipper over his hand and onto George's head. Then George baptized Conrad and the others who were gathered in prayer.

"My friends, we are the first adults to be baptized in this country," said George. "We promise to imitate Christ in everything and to be true disciples. Now let us give thanks to God."

The group of men and women didn't seem to see the strangely-dressed kids in their midst. Only the man outside the room had taken notice of them.

As the adults filed out of the room, Isaac spoke up. "I think it's a good time for a lesson."

"Oh, brother," said Alicia, rolling her eyes.

"Go ahead, preacher man," said Fabio with a smile.

"These new believers who were just baptized came to be known as Anabaptists," Isaac told the others.

"Which means 'rebaptizers,' " said Alicia, "because they re-baptized people who were already baptized as babies. They knew that babies couldn't decide for themselves."

"Being baptized as adults showed that they were breaking away from the old system and joining God's kingdom," added Li.

"You guys sound like Mr. Dirks," said Justin with a grin.

"Oh no! What time is it? We have to get upstairs before Mr. Dirks comes back," said Alicia. "Follow me, and hold on to each other, everyone!"

26

A Great Discovery

The Menno Slick Six were sitting on the blanket in front of the fireplace when Mr. Dirks returned.

"Thank you for waiting so patiently," he said. "I wish all of our museum visitors were as well behaved."

"Mr. Dirks, did you know that your wall over there is . . ." Justin began.

Fabio elbowed Justin and interrupted. "Mr. Dirks, is everything okay in the boys' rest room upstairs?"

"Oh, yes, thank you for asking. Just a little plumbing problem, luckily not a major one. Now, where were we?"

"You were telling us about a baby," said Justin. "Did Conrad and Barbara decide to baptize their baby after all?"

"No," said Mr. Dirks. "They didn't, in spite of threats from the authorities."

"What happened to them?" asked Anna.

"Conrad and George became great preachers and, in spite of much suffering, they remained faithful to Jesus. The authorities put Conrad in prison. He escaped, but had to live the rest of his life running from the police. George was burned at the stake in 1529 in Tyrol, Switzerland."

"When we saw them after their baptism, they said they would be true disciples," said Justin.

"Who did you see baptized?" asked Mr. Dirks with a puzzled look.

"Oh, last Easter several people at our church were baptized," Alicia put in hurriedly, glaring at Justin.

"Mr. Dirks, how many people were killed because of their beliefs?" asked Anna.

"Thousands. Not just Anabaptists, but other Christians too. Our faith history is full of heroes."

"Did that man in the picture behind you die for his beliefs too?" Anna asked, pointing above the bricks. "Who is that?" The picture showed a man sitting at a table with an open book, a feathered pen in his hand. His hair and beard were gray, and a tiny cap sat on his head.

"Anna, that's Menno Simons. The Mennonite Church is named after him. Menno lived in the Netherlands and was one of the greatest Anabaptist leaders. He helped people turn away from violence, and kept the Anabaptist movement going in its most troublesome days."

"How did he help people turn away from violence?" Anna asked.

"A good question, Anna. I can share a story about Menno Simons, if you'd like."

"Yes!" they all replied.

"Okay, let's start with the biggest decision Menno

ever made: Should he remain a priest in the Catholic Church or should he join the Anabaptists who believed as he did, though it meant breaking the law?

"It was a tough decision, because the adult baptizers didn't always agree about what they believed. Most of them believed all war was wrong, but some believed they must fight for the truth. In fact, nearly 200 Anabaptists had taken over a city and defended it with swords.

"Menno finally decided to serve God with the peaceful Anabaptists. He announced his new commitment to Christ and went into hiding with the help of his Anabaptist friends. He spent the next year studying scripture and writing.

"At the end of the year, Menno had to make another important decision. The peace-loving Anabaptists had asked him to be their leader. It was a dangerous and difficult job, and Menno wasn't sure he could do it. He felt like he wasn't wise enough, and his body wasn't strong. The Anabaptists were scattered over a wide area. He said they were like sheep without a shepherd.

"But Menno couldn't refuse. He gave himself completely to God and started to teach and baptize. He visited the scattered churches by night for 25 years and wrote many letters to them. He and his family couldn't live more than half a year in one place, because he was always in danger.

"Some Anabaptists came to be called Mennonites after Menno, to show they were different from 'fighting' Anabaptists. In one of his letters, Menno wrote, 'O beloved reader, our weapons are not swords and spears, but patience, silence, hope, and the Word of God.'

"Well, campers, you're great listeners, but we really need to go," finished Mr. Dirks. "The others will be wondering about us. Can you come back to the museum next week? I'd like to show you more of our treasures. And tell you more of our faith-hero stories."

"I have something to show you, too, Mr. Dirks," said Anna. She felt in her pocket and pulled out the yellowed, creased slip of paper. "It's got weird hand-writing on it."

Anna handed over her precious treasure to Mr. Dirks. "Maybe you can help me . . . I mean us, figure out what it means."

Mr. Dirks adjusted his glasses and held the paper close to his face. Anna watched him closely.

"Where did you get this, Anna?" Mr. Dirk's face was ghostly white, and his lips were trembling.

"I found it in the woods, next to the peace garden at camp," Anna said.

"I think you've found something extremely valu-able, Anna." Mr. Dirks' voice was hoarse with emotion. He took a handkerchief from his pocket, took off his glasses, and slowly wiped them clean as he stared at the bricks in the unfinished fireplace.

"What does the paper say, Mr. Dirks?" Justin asked eagerly, moving closer to Anna.

"And ye shall know the truth, and the truth shall make you free," Mr. Dirks replied slowly. "The words are written in German."

"*That's* why I couldn't read it!" cried Anna.

"It's from the New Testament: John, chapter 8, verse 32," put in Isaac.

"They passed this scripture verse to each other in the forests of Switzerland," Mr. Dirks went on. "Almost 500 years ago."

"Who did?" Alicia asked. "Are you okay, Mr. Dirks?"

"The early Anabaptists." Mr Dirks turned and stared at the fireplace again. "Five hundred years ago . . . Michael and Margareta Sattler, Wilhelm Reublin, George Blaurock, Conrad Grebel . . . 500 years ago."

"Mr. Dirks, we have to get back to the other campers upstairs," Isaac said. "Shall we go ahead? Are you okay? Are you going to stay down here?"

"No, I can't stay down here. I have to make an urgent phone call. I'll explain later."

Mr. Dirks turned and looked at Anna. "Thank you," he said. He raised his hand that held the small, yellowed piece of paper. "You've made a great discovery!"

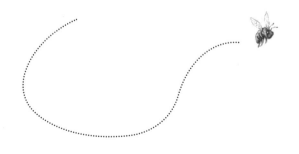

27

Colored Threads
and Unity

Anna will be back today. It's the last day of camp, guys! She said she'd be here." Justin and the other members of the Menno Slick Six were waiting for the counselors to give their familiar words of welcome.

"I hope her visit with her mom at the prison went okay," Li said.

"Has anyone heard from Mr. Dirks?" asked Fabio. "Man, he got weirded out over that little slip of paper."

"Does anyone else think it's kind of strange that we're sitting on army blankets today?" Alicia frowned.

"How do you know they're *army* blankets?" Fabio asked.

"Because they look like army blankets. They're green, and they're made out of coarse material."

"Were you ever in the army?" Isaac joked. " 'Cause I don't know how you could know they're army blankets unless you were in the army and used them."

Alicia rolled her eyes. "Thank goodness this is the last day of camp."

"You don't mean that, do you?" asked Li.

"No, not really. I'm just messing with Isaac's head. Camp's been great this year."

"Even with Anna Bee?" asked Isaac.

"Yes, even with Anna Bee."

"I think Anna Bee's the greatest thing that's happened to us all summer," Justin declared.

"But bro, it's only June. There's still July and August. You might find something else that's the greatest thing by the end of the summer," said Fabio.

"Nope, that's my story, and I'm sticking to it," Justin grinned.

"Welcome to Camp Amani Ya Juu!" the counselors shouted.

"This is the first day of the rest of your lives and the last day of Camp Amani Ya Juu for you," Christina said. "Have you had a good time this week?"

"Yeah!" the campers shouted back.

"We hope you've had lots of fun, but we also hope you've learned some new things about Anabaptist martyrs, Mennonite faith heroes, and peacemakers. Anyone want to share what stood out for you this week?"

"The threads of many colors!" shouted a voice from the edge of the blankets.

"That's Anna Bee!" exclaimed Justin. "I told you she'd come back."

"I'm glad someone remembered the threads," said Jesse, the counselor. "No one ever solved that puzzle at the museum. What do the threads mean to you, Anna? By the way, welcome back. We missed you yesterday."

Anna had caught sight of Justin, waving his hand in the air, and made her way to her friends. She sat in the spot they saved for her in the middle, then jumped back up to answer Jesse's question.

"It takes a lot of colored threads to make a coat of many colors. That's what Justin says, anyway. Mennonites have a lot of colors in their coat," she laughed.

"Black for Alicia and Justin and some of the volunteers with Mennonite Central Committee who worked in Atlanta," she added.

"Hey, I get the thread thing now," Isaac said. "Mennonites are made up of all kinds of people, all colors, not just white with Mennonite ancestors like me."

"Red for Anna Bee and Lawrence Hart and other Native peoples," said Fabio.

"Tan for Fabio and Javier Segura Gonzales and other cool Latinos!" shouted Justin.

"Yellow for me and the painter Lien-Nu Huang and my great-grandmother and great-grandfather Tee Siem Tat," said Li.

"Multi-color for me!" shouted another camper. "And for some of the kids we saw in the video, building the garden shed."

"Me too," said Anna. "I'm red and white. Half

Cherokee, half Irish. That's why my hair's so wild," she joked.

Other campers started sharing what was special to them during camp week.

"I liked planting the peace garden," one said, "and learning about Dan Stuckey, who stood guard with a hoe instead of a gun. That was cool."

"And the treasures we found!" shouted another camper.

"The museum was neat. I liked spending the day there," said another.

Justin raised his hand and stood up. "I liked the castle and meeting Jacques Dosie best of all," he volunteered.

Christina and the other counselors looked puzzled. "Justin, we didn't have Jacques Dosie's story on our list this year. Maybe you read about him in a book?"

"No, Anna and I talked to him. We were in the castle. It was cool, but sad, too."

Alicia and the others were glaring at Justin hard enough to bore holes. "Sit down, Justin!" Alicia hissed, pulling on his shirt.

Christina hesitated a moment. "Uh, thanks for sharing, Justin. Maybe you can help us present Jacques Dosie's story next year. You have a great imagination." The other counselors nodded.

"Why are we sitting on army blankets today?" asked one of the campers.

Alicia looked at Isaac and rolled her eyes. "I told you they were army blankets."

"I was wondering when someone was going to

bring that up," Jesse responded. He looked at Anna. "Still okay if I share what happened yesterday?" Anna nodded her head.

"Yesterday, campers, something cool happened. Jennifer Snyder is one of our college classmates, and she's involved in an important prison ministry with her church. She visits women prisoners each month in a military prison 70 miles from here. Well, yesterday Anna Bee was also visiting someone at the prison."

Jesse looked at Anna. "Want to tell the rest of the story, Anna?"

"Sure," she said, standing up. "My mom is in prison there."

Some of the campers gasped.

"She's there because she refused to obey orders to torture people," Anna continued. "My dad and brother and me met Jennifer at the prison yesterday. She's nice. She was visiting my mom. After I talked to Mom for awhile, Jennifer and I went to get a snack together. We talked about camp and stuff. She asked me about the quilts and said she helped piece some of them. I told her my mom liked quilts and that she even had one from Ireland."

"I'd like to see a quilt from Ireland," Justin said softly.

Anna smiled at him and continued. "Jennifer came up with the idea to use army blankets at camp today, as a way to help me tell all of you about my mom and where she is."

Anna looked at Jesse. "You can finish the story, okay?"

Jesse took up the story. "So Jennifer called me, and I thought her idea was super. I talked to the other counselors, and we all agreed it would be a great ending to a great week."

"I still don't get it," Alicia said to Isaac. "Mennonites don't believe in joining the military, so why are we sitting on army blankets?"

"Listen up, campers!" Christina's voice interrupted Alicia's thoughts. "Our plan for today was to cut up the quilts you've been sitting on all week and start piecing together smaller quilts. Now we'll also add strips of army blankets. We have enough fabric to make several quilts. So here's the deal. You get to choose where the quilts will go when they're finished."

"Got any ideas?" Jesse asked.

"Anna's mom, in prison!" several campers shouted.

"The Union Mission Shelter for the homeless!" another yelled.

"The Women's Shelter," Li added.

"The Hispanic Medical Center," said Fabio. "Moms and dads and kids can cuddle up in a blanket while they wait."

"How about other women in prison?" Anna said.

"And men, too," added another camper.

"Are any kids in prison?" asked Justin.

"No, dude, they don't put kids in prison," one of the campers replied.

"Well, there are young people in special correctional schools," Jesse said. "It's not prison, but they're locked up."

"Let's send a quilt there, too," Alicia said.

"Okay, how many quilts does that make?" asked Jesse.

"At least four," replied Isaac. "But if you add other people in prison and teens in correctional schools, that's lots more."

"What about giving one to the children's ward of the hospital?" Li asked.

"How about some for the old men in the Veteran's Hospital?" asked Anna. "I bet they get really lonely and sad."

"These are all great suggestions, campers," Christina said. "Do you think we can piece together six-plus quilts today?"

"Yeah!" shouted the campers.

"How hard is it?" asked Justin.

"It takes skill and a lot of time," replied Christina.

"We could have a lock-in and work all night," suggested Anna.

"You kids are always a step ahead of us counselors," Jesse said, smiling at Anna. "How 'bout a lock-in, campers?"

"Yeah!" they shouted back.

"Okay, here's the plan," said Christina. "We'll check with your parents and arrange for a lock-in weekend at the Mennonite History Museum. Mr. Dirks has some extra rooms for special occasions."

"In the basement?" Anna asked.

"I don't know about the basement, but I know we can use some rooms on the main floor," said Christina. "I'll call Mr. Dirks before we start our next activity and check for dates it might work."

"Cool!" said Fabio and Justin, giving each other a high-five.

"We may not finish all the quilts that weekend, but we'll get a good start," said Christina. "Today we'll work on one quilt, with a little help from some friends."

Five volunteers showed up later that morning, bringing supplies, sewing machines, and a quilting frame. Every person helped put together pieces of the quilts and army blankets.

Later, the proud campers looked at their handi-work. "This is our Camp Amani Ya Juu unity quilt," Christina said. "It's a quilt of many-colored threads, of smooth and rough fabrics. It represents all types of people. All are welcome to sit together on this quilt."

"Like the two-colored table we found in the muse-um," said Alicia. "All are welcome at God's table. And all are welcome on God's quilt."

"This can be a reminder of our week together," added Christina. "A reminder of heroes and martyrs, of peacemakers and followers of Jesus. Some gave their lives for their faith. Some spoke up for what they believed even in the face of death. Some serve today, all over the world. Thank you, campers, for being part of our awesome time together."

28

Celebrations and Revelations

L et the celebrations begin!" Andi and Tim shouted as they ran through the campers, handing out streamers and noise makers. They had brought musical instruments, too. "Anyone ready for a peace feast party?"

"Did you say *feast*?" shouted Justin. "Yes!"

The campers scattered, picking up guitars, drums, and tambourines.

"Gather 'round, campers. There will be music; there will be food; there will be surprises," announced Tim.

Isaac started playing a guitar. Fabio and Justin beat on drums. Li, Alicia, and Anna shook tambourines. Other campers found instruments, too. One even tried an Australian didjerido.

"These kids are good!" Tim exclaimed. "Maybe we should start a Camp Amani Ya Juu band."

"Let's get the quilts finished first," Andi said, smiling.

"Campers! Attention, please," yelled Tim. "Some

of the treasure-clue winners haven't received their prizes yet. While we serve the food, we'll award the final prizes."

The counselors brought out watermelons, strawberry sundaes, butternut squash muffins, potato sticks, and raw broccoli. "The foods used to make these delicacies will be growing in the peace garden you planted this week," Andi told the campers. "We'll use some of the food for camp celebrations, and we'll donate some to the community food bank. Thanks for your hard work in the garden."

"Coming through, coming through!" Tim shouted as he carried a big crock above his head. "This prize goes to Justin Aduma—a crock full of your favorite food."

"Cheese!" everyone shouted. Justin's smile was as big as a half moon.

"The next prize goes to Anna Bee," announced Andi. "She found the headdress feathers in the Lawrence Hart quilt. Remember the puzzle? 'Find the match to the feather. Whoever solves the puzzle gets to wear a different sweater.'"

"It's too hot to wear a sweater," said one of the campers.

"That's why we're substituting a T-shirt," said Andi. "Anna, because it took a lot of guts for you to come to camp this week without knowing anyone, I present you with a special T-shirt."

Anna took the T-shirt and held it up for all to see. It proclaimed, "Peace takes guts!" and featured the faces of six peacemakers.

"That's Cheyenne Peace Chief Lawrence Hart," Anna said, pointing to one of the faces. "But who are the others?"

"Campers, can you help us out?" asked Andi.

"That's Caesar Chavez, a Mexican-American who helps migrant workers," Fabio said.

"That's someone from Women in Black, a women's peace organization," said another camper.

"That's Sojourner Truth, an African-American preacher who spoke out against slavery," added Alicia.

"And that's Philip Berrigan, a Catholic priest and man of peace," said a camper.

"That one is Maeykyn Wens, a sixteenth-century Anabaptist martyr," said Isaac.

"Is that Adriaen and Hans' mother?" asked Justin.

"Yes, it is," said Andi, surprised. "You must have been reading a lot about the martyrs."

Alicia pinched Justin's arm to keep him from saying more. "Is there another prize still left to give away?" she asked, changing the subject.

"Yes, there's one more," said Andi. "Fabio Flores solved the puzzle of the cloth, so he gets to dance with Isaac Thomas Roth."

The campers screamed and laughed.

"Now wait a minute. Don't get too excited," said Fabio, putting up his hands. "I'm going to teach Isaac how to dance the salsa. And I'm opening up the dance lesson to all of you. So start the music!"

Tim turned on a CD player, and soon the campers and counselors were learning to salsa in the middle of the remaining blankets.

"If only my great-grandpa could see me now," Isaac said, laughing breathlessly. "He'd never believe a Mennonite from Russia would be dancing in the middle of a church camp with Latinos, Asians, Native peoples, and African-Americans."

"And Irish," added Anna.

"All are welcome on the dance floor, bro. All are welcome!" shouted Fabio.

"And all are welcome to follow Jesus' way of peace," added Anna.

Alicia and Isaac smiled at her.

"My mom can pick you and your brother up on Sunday, if you want," said Li.

"Yeah, thanks," Anna said, nodding.

"Anna, can you come to my house tomorrow night? The others already said yes. We could watch your video," said Fabio.

"Sure," agreed Anna.

"Dad and Justin and I are going to Joyland tomorrow afternoon. They have a cool roller coaster. Want to come?" asked Alicia.

"You bet!" said Anna.

"Anna Bee! Anna Bee!" Mr. Dirks was sprinting toward the campers from the parking lot. He stopped in front of Anna and waved a piece of paper in the air.

"Anna," he said, breathing hard, "I just received this fax from Europe. A museum in Switzerland is interested in the piece of paper you found in the woods. The director's flying here in two weeks to look at it, and he wants to talk to the person who found it. Can you meet with us?"

"Yes!" said Anna. "Can Justin and Alicia, and Isaac and Li and Fabio come too? Please?"

"Well, I don't see why not," answered Mr. Dirks.

"Um, there's something else I haven't told you about," Anna said, reaching into her pocket and taking out the weathered pouch from the forest. Inside were the old map, the strange stamps, and the tarnished silver key. She handed them to Mr. Dirks. "Can you help us find out more about this stuff, too?"

Mr. Dirks looked a bit white again, but smiled at Anna. "I'll certainly try," he said. "I think you, your friends and I have lots of adventures ahead of us."

Justin slipped away from the others and walked to a nearby tree. Leaning against the trunk, he looked around the camp. The Camp Amani Ya Juu unity quilt hung on a stand in the midst of the campers. Peace feast foods covered one end of a long table. Streamers lay scattered about the lawn, and campers were dancing on blankets.

He turned his head and gazed at the mysterious bridge in the distance, remembering all the awesome things that had happened at camp that week. Then he remembered something his dad had said, about God using wayward bees.

He looked around for Anna Bee. She was laughing and dancing, in the middle of a group of kids. She looked toward him and waved. Justin smiled and waved back.

"God really *did* use those wayward bees," he said to himself, his face lighting up in the biggest smile ever.

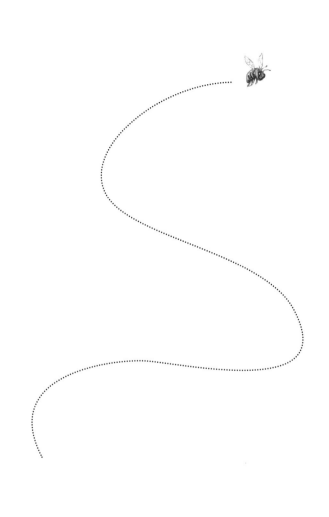

Not the End Yet

I f *Finding Anna Bee* helped you find out more about Anabaptists, then the book accomplished its mission.

Learn more about Anabaptist beliefs and heroes and other interesting facts by reading the following Factoids and Figures. And be sure to check out the resources listed.

Factoids and Figures

1. Honey bees are usually gentle creatures who mind their own business. They are attracted to bright colors, but cannot see red. They were brought to the United States and Canada from Europe in the 1600s.

2. There really is an Amani Ya Juu unity quilt. Amani Ya Juu is a training project in sewing and marketing for African women who have been affected by wars and ethnic conflicts. The women have learned to work together because of their faith in God. Check it out at www.amaniafrica.org. The web site's colors are very peaceful.

3. The name Justin means "fair-minded and true."

4. The *Popol Vuh* is a real Mayan book.

5. Felix Manz was the first Anabaptist martyr. You can read more about his death at the Mennonite Church USA Historical Committee's website, www.mcusa-archives.org.

6. Two books that include information about Maeyken Wens are *On Fire for Christ* by Dave and Neta Jackson and *Mirror of the Martyrs* by John S. Oyer and Robert S. Kreider.

7. The words the kids sang with Adriaen Wens on page 53 are from "The Servant Song" by Richard Gillard. Copyright © Scripture in Song/Maranatha Music/ASCAP (All rights administered by Music Services). Used by permission.

8. For more details about Jacques Dosie, read "The Lady and the Lad" in *On Fire for Christ*.

9. The Chinese *tangram* is a centuries-old test of creative possibilities. Made up of seven geometric pieces *(five triangles, a square, and a parallelogram)*, the tangram can be arranged to show over 300 characters, including people, letters, boats, and animals.

10. You can read about Tee Siem Tat and his wife and how they became Mennonite in *The Mennonite Story* by Rudy Baergen.

11. You can read the story of Ted Studebaker on the Church of the Brethren Network website at www.cob-net.org.

12. There are several Mennonite history museums and historical societies. Check them out at http://info.mennolink.org

13. The character of Mr. Ben Dirks is based on Mr. Ray Dirks, curator at the Mennonite Heritage Centre in Winnipeg, Manitoba, but most of the story is made up.

14. You can order "Peace Takes Guts" T-shirts at http://peace.mennolink.org

15. *Amigo* means "friend" in Spanish.

16. *Mi casa* means "my house" in Spanish.

17. *Hombrecito* is Spanish for "little man."

The Author

Cindy Snider lives in Wichita, Kansas, with her two dogs, Spanky and Maddie. She enjoys writing fiction and nonfiction for children.

As part of Cindy's research, she reads about time travel and quantum physics, studies Anabaptist history and theology, and plans travel adventures with nieces and nephews. She also writes for *The Wichita Eagle*'s faith and values section and for Mennonite Church USA's online peace postings for youth. A former communications director for MC USA, she has written for children's magazines and the devotional magazine, *Rejoice!*. Cindy attends Mennonite Church of the Servant, Wichita.